DON'T NEVER SHOOT SHORT

KENT F. FRATES

BridgewayBooks

Don't Never Shoot Short
Published by Bridgeway Books
P.O. Box 80107
Austin, Texas 78758

For more information about our books, please write to us, call
512.478.2028, or visit our website at www.bridgewaybooks.net.

Library of Congress Control Number: 2007923454

ISBN-13: 978-1-933538-89-1
ISBN-10: 1-933538-89-9

This is a work of fiction. All of the characters and events portrayed
in this book are fictional, and any resemblance to real people or
incidents is purely coincidental.

10 9 8 7 6 5 4 3 2 1

CHAPTER 1

It was an ugly day in an ugly time of year. Western Oklahoma in the early spring is gray and brown—a gray sky and dormant, brown fields. There is no color, and my mood was similar.

I was already awake when the phone rang. As a part-time deputy sheriff, part-time process server, and part-time oil and gas landman, I spend a lot of time in courthouses, but very little time in court. This day was an exception. I was due in Cordell, the county seat of Washita County, at 9:00 a.m. to testify about my attempts to serve a summons in a foreclosure action brought by the Cordell Bank against Leo Morford.

The telephone call came from Mad Mike, the proud owner of Mad Mike's Crop Dusting Service. "Wake up, Snake. Drop your jock and grab your socks, we're going to Mexico. We'll catch some bass, smoke some grass, and chase some ass."

"First of all, what are you doing up this early? Second, what will Long Tall Sally say? And third, I have to be in court in Cordell at nine o'clock over this freemen deal."

"Long Tall Sally's gone back to her husband, and from what I hear, testifying against those guys is not particularly healthy in the first place."

"Which husband—not Freight Train?" I responded.

"Yes, Freight Train. As in, 'Don't fuck with Freight Train.'"

"In that case, you're looking for a new girlfriend, and if I'm not in Cordell at 9:00 a.m., I'll be looking for a new job."

"Well, okay, maybe I should get some sleep before I fly, anyway. I've been up all night worrying about losing Sally."

"You've never lost sleep over any woman, Mike. What worries you is Freight Train."

Freight Train was the biggest, toughest man in the oil fields. No one knew where he came from. He appeared one day on a well in West Texas with no known past. Like Paul Bunyan, his origins were obscure, but his deeds were legendary. He spoke little, but did the work of at least two men. Before long he was a toolpusher himself and then the drilling superintendent for Big Chief Drilling Company, one of the most respected companies in the Oklahoma and Texas oil patch.

The stories regarding Freight Train were myriad, some true and some fantasy. One known to be true occurred in Louisiana, when Big Chief was having trouble with a rash of workers' compensation claims. Concerned about safety procedures and the cost of workers' compensation insurance, Freight Train was sent to investigate the many unexplained claims.

He arrived at a well, somewhere near Lafayette, unannounced. Near the well site he observed one of the crew with an axe in his right hand and his left hand against a tree. Repeatedly, the man drew the axe back as if to strike a blow, but then dropped it to his side without striking. Freight Train approached the crew member and asked what was happening. The man advised that, in Louisiana, if you lost just the tip of an index finger, you were totally, permanently disabled, drew insurance for the rest of your life, and never had to work again, but that he just couldn't get up the courage to cut off his own finger. "No problem," Freight Train replied and, with no hesitation, picked up the axe and cut off the man's finger. It is reported that workers' compensation claims virtually disappeared for Big Chief.

"Well, Mike, I like your idea, but perhaps we should wait until you get over your grief from the loss of Sally. On the other hand, if you think Freight Train is going to hold a grudge, I suspect Mexico may not be far enough away."

"All right, you smart-ass son of a bitch, see if I care if the freemen make you a target." With that, Mike hung up abruptly. Based on past experience, I might hear from him again in five minutes, five days, or five weeks. But he would turn up again, unless the pot, the whiskey, or Freight Train interfered.

Being fully awake, I showered, shaved, got dressed, pulled my aging Jeep Cherokee out of the driveway, and headed for Cordell. On the way I stopped at a Conoco station for coffee in a Styrofoam cup, which tasted vaguely like watery chicken soup. The day grew no better, as a chilly forty-mile-per-hour wind blew in from the North. The traffic was light, but of course the traffic was always light—except during harvest, when the combines clogged the road on the way from one wheat field to the next.

I came into town from the North on the road that led from the interstate through the almost colorless day. I passed the boarded-up car dealerships that boomed during the oil boom and busted in the oil bust, and then passed the two banks that failed, and the one that didn't—because my father preferred to die of pride rather than let it happen. I kept on toward the golden dome of the courthouse, an architectural throwback to that period when authority meant stability, and people looked to the law to deal out justice, not just money to someone who felt victimized by the least slight society might offer.

Set in the town square, solid and lasting, the courthouse still had an operating clock tower. It was built in 1911 to replace its predecessor, which was destroyed by fire. Arson was suspected, and given the history of the Washita county seat, the suspicion may have been justified. Cordell was not the first county seat of Washita County. In 1900, a group favoring Cordell stole the county records from the then county seat of Cloud Chief. A mob from Cloud Chief was subdued only by the prospect of an appeal to the territorial government in Guthrie. A young attorney named Murphy carried the appeal to Guthrie by horseback. When news reached Cloud Chief that the appeal had been filed too late for legal action, Murphy was tarred, feathered, and run out of town.

I entered the courthouse through the street door walking on the worn-out linoleum that covered the lobby. I passed the ancient Coke machine and a dozen or so welfare recipients sitting on wooden benches, waiting to inquire about food stamps and aid to dependent children. The smell was musty and stale from years of the sweat of many people—not quite clean. It was a place populated by every level of society, from lawyers, judges, and landmen to common thieves and unemployed drifters, all summoned or dragged into court for all the reasons the law might imagine. Somehow I always felt comfortable in the courthouse, as though it was my natural habitat.

At the top of the stairs was the courtroom of Judge Don Ed Roberts, my last best friend. A deputy sheriff was posted at the door and the sheriff and three other deputies were in the courtroom. It was the entire force, except for the jailer, consisting of Sheriff "Chubby" Checker and his deputies, "Red," "Smokey," "Lookout," and "Speedy." A nickname was mandatory for employment as a deputy sheriff in Oklahoma, and I'd never heard of a deputy who didn't have one. When I came on the force I was immediately identified by my old nickname of "Snake," adopted as a small-town high school quarterback whose hero was Ken "Snake" Stabler of the Oakland Raiders. The deputies were all armed with side arms, night sticks, and mace—an uncommon display of force for what was usually a sleepy and routine court proceeding.

"Hey, Boss, why the heavy artillery?"

"Judge Roberts called out the troops. Old Morford's mean as hell and crazy, and this guy that's coaching him is one of these militia kooks. Since the Murrah Building bombing, everybody's squirrelly when it comes to these cats."

Just then the door to the courtroom swung open, and Morford and a man unknown to me entered the court. Red stuck his head through the door and waved an okay to the sheriff, meaning he had frisked them and found no weapons. They took a seat on the front row of the spectators' benches. Morford, tall, stooped-shouldered, burned brown, and wrinkled by the sun with big, loose-hanging farmer's hands and black, stringy hair, was dressed in clean blue jeans, cracked and worn cowboy boots, and a long-sleeved, white shirt buttoned at the neck. He looked uncomfortable. The man with him was the perfect picture of paramilitary correctness—crew cut, thick neck, bulging arms and shoulders, and dressed in clean khakis with spit-shined combat boots, ready for war against the system.

Floyd Meeker, the Cordell Bank's lawyer who would call me as a witness, motioned me over for a brief conversation. Floyd was the dean of the western Oklahoma bar. He'd come over from Clinton himself and not sent his son as he would have usually done. Pink-faced, cherubic, and in his sixties, he was known for his meticulous—some said nit-picking—knowledge of legal procedure. No *t* was too small to cross, nor *i* too small to dot. He could turn a one-hour hearing into a day long ordeal, but in all his years of practice he had only had one case reversed on appeal—a black mark he never acknowledged.

"All rise. The District Court of Washita County is now in session," the judge's ancient bailiff proclaimed as the judge took the bench.

My friend, Don Ed, was a most improbable looking character for a judge. He looked like a burned-out hippie hunting for some good mushrooms. He was of medium height, slightly built, but stringy and tough, like the rodeo cowboy he had been. His head was crowned with a thinning shock of long, wispy hair that descended to his shoulders, more appropriate for Woodstock, or San Francisco, than Cordell.

A true anachronism, Don Ed was a liberal in the midst of conservatives. He'd been driven from his criminal practice by a heart attack after some twenty-five years spent defending those accused of every crime in the books. Starting as a public defender, he'd turned into a roving ACLU lawyer, traveling the southwest to fight against the death penalty. After the attack, he had been appointed as district judge by a democratic governor. In spite of the conservative nature of his constituents, he won later elections simply because he was the best and smartest lawyer in that part of the state, and more importantly, "a good ol' boy." Don Ed had a friendly greeting for everyone and might be seen drinking coffee with his pals at the café or sipping a beer at the Fourth of July barbecue. He was a person people just flat-out liked, but in his courtroom there was no question who was in charge.

"The court will call the case of *Cordell Bank v. Morford*. The lawyers will please enter their appearance for the record," stated the bailiff.

"The plaintiff is present and ready to proceed. I am Floyd Meeker, the plaintiff's attorney."

At which point the paramilitary character opened an attaché case and extracted a voluminous looking legal document. He stood, addressed the court, and in a booming voice began to read from a prepared script.

"I am General Sherman. Mr. Morford challenges the jurisdiction of this illegal, unconstitutional, and bankrupt court. He moves to dismiss this case and return it to the common-law court of his peers. I am not a lawyer, but I am a freeman and his counselor at law under the common law of the land."

However long his prepared speech might have been, it went no further. The judge pounded his gavel and interrupted. "Mr. Sherman, sit down. You are not a lawyer, and you cannot practice law before this court. Mr. Morford can hire a lawyer, or he can represent himself, but you have no authority to represent him. You may stay as a spectator or leave, but I will not recognize you further. Let the record show that Mr. Morford is present in person and without counsel," the judge continued. "Mr. Meeker, please call your first witness."

"Thank you, Judge. The plaintiff will call Deputy Sheriff Ken Frasier," Floyd intoned.

As I walked toward the witness stand, I could see the general furiously whispering into Morford's ear. Before I could reach the stand, Morford rose hesitantly to his feet and spoke.

"Judge, I object to the jury diction of the court."

"Your objection is noted and overruled," the judge replied. "Please proceed, Mr. Meeker."

Floyd then began to question me about how I went about serving the summons on Morford for the plaintiff bank. It was an event I wasn't likely to forget. Under Floyd's questioning, I recited how I went to Morford's farm, crossed a cattle guard onto his land, and drove up the road toward his house, passing posted "No Trespassing" signs, until I came to a locked gate some hundred feet from the front of Morford's farmhouse. Here I was met by a pack of barking dogs. I stopped my car, got out, and tried the gate, which was securely locked. Before I could reenter my car, Morford appeared from his house armed with a shotgun. He marched toward me in a threatening manner and told me to, "Get the hell off the property." However threatening Morford was physically, he had made his first mistake legally. I was able to throw the summons at his feet, and even though he stated, "I don't want your damn papers," he was, according to Oklahoma law, served, and the foreclosure suit against him had begun.

Floyd led me painstakingly through every minute detail of my experience, being particularly careful to cover the date, the time, and the identity of Morford.

Before I could fully finish my testimony, General Sherman rose from his seat and in a stentorian voice proclaimed, "This illegal court is powerless to affect the person or property of freemen. It is unauthorized by the Republic and its rulings are null and void."

As the judge banged his gavel and turned to admonish Sherman, the general went on to say, "You don't need to address me further, Judge. Mr. Morford and I are leaving." At which point he and Morford marched out of the courtroom.

"Let the record show the defendant has voluntarily removed himself from the courtroom and is no longer present," the judge said. "You may continue, Mr. Meeker."

Floyd then finished questioning me and called a vice president of the bank as a witness to identify the note and mortgage and to establish Morford's default and the amount owed to the bank. Don Ed then entered an order of foreclosure against Morford, which would

7

ultimately lead to a sheriff's sale of the property. He ordered Floyd to serve the order on Morford and then paused and, looking at me with a smile he could not quite contain, said, "Oh, Floyd, the order can be served by certified mail. No personal service is necessary."

After the hearing I saw Floyd talking on his cell phone, no doubt informing Duane Lucas, the owner of the bank, of the outcome. Lucas lived in Elk City and was rich by any measure. There weren't many rich people in Elk City, but it didn't really matter where Lucas lived. He would have amassed a fortune if he lived on Mars, his life being fired by the purest form of total greed.

Lucas started with a wholesale gasoline distributorship. He soon owned a small gasoline refinery, and then auto dealerships, banks, and newspapers. The profits of his many businesses were plowed into oil and gas ventures and land. Lucas was a land hog, sucking up farms and ranches all over Oklahoma. His tactics were ruthless, using his bank to make loans on valuable properties whose owners had dubious credit, and then foreclosing and obtaining the land for a fraction of its value. He was nasty, litigious, and totally without shame. Virtually everyone he ever dealt with hated him for good reason. Small of stature, he was a dapper dresser who affected a phony charm even when inserting the knife into some helpless debtor or business adversary. His office in his bank in Elk City was arranged so that his desk and chair were raised above the level of the floor to look down on visitors, like a throne. After a conversation with Lucas, all I could ever think about was washing my hands. To put it in Oklahoma terms, Duane Lucas was one sorry son of a bitch.

Like every legitimate businessman in the state, my dad, M.B., despised Lucas, who was the antithesis of M.B.'s unyielding integrity. In the end, dealing with Lucas was what killed my father.

CHAPTER 2

The next day the sheriff and I walked across the street to the café. Located in a dilapidated storefront across from the courthouse, it was a typical small-town café, with torn and soiled booths, Formica tables, and a counter with six stools. The name of the café was Amazing Grazing, but it was known simply as "the café." The oil boom and the subsequent bust hadn't affected the food or the coffee much either way. It was consistently low-mediocre, just barely good enough to eat or drink. The café was popular, mostly because it was the only place open downtown. During the boom it had been crowded with landmen and lawyers who were checking titles at the courthouse and then racing around the county offering to pay outrageous bonuses for oil and gas leases on unproven acreage. Now it was populated by the usual small-town crowd—employees from the court clerk's office, farmers and ranchers in town on business, and the few businessmen who had survived the economy's collapse.

You know, these people remind me of ticks," the sheriff said as we entered the front door. His voice always disconcerted me, as he sounded like Tom Waits, even though his looks justified the nickname "Chubby."

"What are you talking about?"

"Well, no one really knows how ticks survive the winter, but they sure as hell do. These people somehow managed to survive times that should have run 'em off or killed 'em."

"It did kill M.B.," I pointed out. "I guess he was a little too human, or a little too proud."

"I'll tell you one thing, Snake. Your dad was one fine old man."

"Maybe so, but dead is still dead. I wish he'd died a little happier."

"Enough of that depressing bullshit, son. Let's talk about football. What do you think about the Sooners' chances to recruit that big lineman over at Hobart? He's some kind of hoss."

We sat down with one of the county commissioners and two local farmers, and the conversation turned to the weather and local politics. I looked at the last stool at the counter, and my mind drifted away to another time, when my dad occupied that place every day at 12:15 sharp. He walked down from Cordell National Bank, which he owned, standing as straight and tall as the old Army captain he had been in 1945. Always dressed in a dark suit and red tie, he sat in the same place every day and read the *Wall Street Journal* while he ate the plate lunch. His routine never varied, except during quail season or on fall Saturdays when he drove with me to Norman to watch his beloved Oklahoma University football team thrash the hell out of some over-matched opponent or struggle for victory with a tough Nebraska or Colorado team.

I don't always remember exactly what those games looked like, but I will never forget what it felt like to sit next to M.B. in the same seats year after year and escape the rigid, structured world he had made for us at home. It was there I decided to be a football player and then a quarterback. And it was there that I began to observe my father as a person, not just as the authoritarian figure that ruled my life.

Those fall Saturdays were so enjoyable because they gave me an escape from M.B.'s style of parenthood. He got his training as a father in the U.S. Army. He commanded my life as he would have any private in his company. This meant not only strict rules, but also strict and certain discipline. In my younger years, this included some mighty spankings—always one spank, always hard, and always with his belt. The punishment was delivered without relish, rage, or passion, but merely as the lesson I needed—caused by my acts, not his. He was as dispassionate in his duties as disciplinarian as he was in his duties as president of the bank. Rules were important, and violating them was unacceptable. A good soldier should know better, and if not, pay the penalty. It didn't always work, but it did make me craftier when it came to avoiding M.B.'s directives. I got very hard to catch.

My mother died when I was an infant, and I had no memory of her. M.B. dedicated what was left of his life, after the bank, to my raising. It was probably more his sense of duty than it was any affection for a small toddler, but as the years went by I think he came to love me, as much out of pride in his ability to supervise my upbringing as anything he saw in me as a person. The bank came first and then me, although the things he truly cared about would make a pretty short list.

M.B.'s design for my life included school, work, and little else, with the exception of sports. He was a sucker for sports, any kind. Having never been an athlete himself, he was impressed by my abilities and later achievements. Sports were my escape and recreation, so I played them all—basketball, baseball, track, tennis, and most of all, football.

"Snake, come to the party, Boy," the sheriff stated, rousing me from my daydreaming. "We need to get back to work. You and Red have to take that guy down to the state prison at Granite."

"You mean Cedric? That son of a bitch is through and through mean—why me, Lord?"

"The rest of the boys are busy, and I've got to send two men with that creep."

"Hell, two may not be enough."

"Oh yeah, you and Red are plenty. Now get your ass in gear."

CHAPTER 3

As I waited at my desk, I continued to daydream about my past and how I managed to end up back in Cordell.

As the quarterback, and later the star of the high school football team, I was clearly good enough to play in college, but OU ran the wishbone, and my strength was as a drop-back passer. Big enough at 6'3" and over 200 pounds, to be a runner, I was simply too slow to fit into a wishbone offense. Besides, I loved to throw.

Offers came in from Tulsa, Houston, and Arkansas, but due to M.B.'s prodding me into studying and making good grades, I was able to get into Stanford. The lure of the west coast and the bright lights of San Francisco made it an easy decision. Even M.B. was happy as he visualized me getting a good education, regardless of how I faired on the football field.

When I got to Stanford, I quickly figured out I wasn't the greatest quarterback in the world. Small-town Oklahoma football didn't exactly prepare me for Division I play in the Pac-10. The coach ran a complicated pro offense, patterned after the 49er's west-coast style, with a lot of passing from multiple formations and receivers seemingly going in all directions at once. It took me a while to catch on to the system, but by the middle of the season I had worked up to backup quarterback and the holder on field goals and extra points, which at least allowed me to get into the games. I played a few minutes in routs, when we were either so far behind, or ahead, that the outcome was not in doubt.

Being second string didn't bother me the first year, but after two years I was sure I was playing behind a quarterback with less ability. After three years my frustration really began to show, always "contending for the job," but never quite ending up as the starter. The coach was never short of a reason. I was a little bit too slow, wasn't a "leader," or whatever. In reality I just didn't like to be coached and resisted authority. It showed, and the coach didn't like my attitude.

My desire to have a good time didn't help either. My attitude toward the coach and my inclination to party were probably a reaction to M.B.'s strict upbringing. San Francisco and its jazz and blues clubs beckoned, and I hit the books just enough to get by with a B-average. Thus, my football career was limited to brief appearances and an occasional game, or part of a game, when the starting quarterback was hurt. So I meandered through four years largely unknown and unrecognized. That is until my senior season.

Somehow we made it to the Rose Bowl. We lost two conference games, but so did USC, and we managed to squeak out a victory over the hated Trojans in the Coliseum. We won our last game against Cal, but only because their best receiver dropped a sure touchdown pass in the end zone with less than a minute left in the game, and that sent us to the Rose Bowl.

When we got to Pasadena, I treated it largely as a vacation. Knowing I wouldn't figure in the game to any great extent, I enjoyed Disneyland, the Hollywood studios, the parties, and the great meals the Rose Bowl threw for the team.

We were playing Michigan, and they were heavy favorites, having won the Big-10 and only losing one game to Notre Dame. It never rains in Southern California, but it did on the day of the game. The field was muddy, the ball slippery, and the scoring was low. We were down 20–14 on our own twenty-yard line and had the ball with one minute and fifty-eight seconds left in the game. I remember the exact time because that was the moment that Michigan's all-American linebacker broke through and hammered our quarterback, knocking him unconscious and out of the game. It was third down and nine, so when I came off the sidelines there wasn't even the opportunity to try a running play to get into the rhythm of the game. The coach gave me the play, which of course was a pass. Everybody in the huddle was covered with mud and pretty much exhausted, except for me. I called the play, and one of the linemen said, "Don't screw it up, Okie." Reassuring, under the circumstances.

The Michigan defense sent two linebackers at me, trying to put on pressure and assuming I would rattle. But I hit the tight end over the middle for twelve yards and a first down with a perfect pass. The next play was an out route to the wide receiver. As he cut to the sideline he fell down on the slippery field, and the ball went wide and out of bounds. That gave the coach a chance to send in another play. As I faded back I could see one of the big Michigan tackles slip his block and come straight at me. I managed to sidestep and look down the field just as our best receiver got by the Michigan safety. What was to be the only important pass of my otherwise lackluster career hit the wide receiver in stride forty yards down the field, and he outraced the Michigan secondary into the end zone. We kicked the extra point and, after holding off a furious Michigan attempt at a comeback, won the game 21–20.

As years went by, my career became more and more exaggerated and more and more successful. From merely playing on the team, I became the starting quarterback, and then the hero of the Rose Bowl, and finally an all-American. In truth, all I had was my fifteen minutes of fame, although it really lasted only one. I did have something to tell my grandchildren about and the basis for a lot of good lies at cocktail parties. In the meantime I had a chance to get a good education and met a wide range of smart and interesting characters who became scientists, doctors, lawyers, prominent businessmen, and noted white-collar criminals.

CHAPTER 4

The prisoner Red and I were to transport to Granite was Cedric Hoesteder. Cedric was going down for the third time for multiple drug convictions. He was an armed robber who also ran a meth lab out of a trailer near the small town of Burns Flat. He probably wouldn't have been caught if his lab hadn't blown up one Friday night. Cedric survived, although he did receive some bad burns. His common-law wife wasn't so lucky and died in the fire.

Cedric was crazy. He was also mean. A big, stringy-looking man sporting prison tattoos of a rough-looking swastika on his shoulder and barbed wire around his neck and wrists. He had long, black, greasy hair and a black beard. He looked bad, he smelled bad, and he was bad. The trip to Granite took less than two hours, but I wasn't looking forward to it.

Red and I and the jailer cuffed Cedric's hands and put a leg chain on his ankles. He didn't resist, but once manacled, turned with an evil grin on his face and spat onto the jailer's clean shirt.

"That's for givin' that nigger his supper before me."

"Keep your damn mouth shut, Cedric," Red stated as he laid his nightstick sharply across Cedric's shin.

"Watch yourself, pig fucker," was Cedric's reply.

"Come on, boys, no more fun. We're going to Granite," I said as I jerked Cedric's ankle chain and pushed him toward the jail door.

Red's nickname wasn't based on the color of his hair. He was dubbed Red because no one had ever seen him without a big chaw of Red Man chewing tobacco jammed into the corner of his mouth.

As soon as we got out of the jail, Red let fly a great arching shot of tobacco juice, which landed next to Cedric's shoe and splattered his pant leg. Cedric snarled "asshole" at Red, who only smiled benignly.

We got Cedric into the car without further incident and headed for the state prison at Granite, some fifty miles southwest. The prison got its name from the town where it was located, which was situated around a granite quarry. Little existed there besides the prison and a business that made gravestones out of granite. There was even a huge rock pile of granite on the prison grounds. All those songs and jokes about working on the rock pile were true when it came to doing time at Granite. It was remote and located where the terrain and weather were hard—hot in the summer under a dry, relentless sun, and in winter, buffeted by cold prairie winds blowing down from the north. It was a hard place to do hard time, and Cedric knew it well.

We were transporting Cedric in an old highway patrol cruiser the sheriff had talked the county into buying for road trips. It had been repainted and fitted with a heavy wire screen that divided the back seat from the front. I drove since Red was a notoriously slow driver.

As we pulled out of town on the road that aimed out across the flat plains and endless sky of western Oklahoma, Red began to tell old war stories about Cedric. It seems Red had arrested him at least once before—that time on an armed robbery charge. He caught Cedric by surprising him coming out of one of the few convenience stores Cedric had ever been in and not robbed, and was able to make the arrest without serious problems, even though Cedric had been armed with a pistol, a derringer, and a spring-activated, switchblade hunting knife. Red also said Cedric had been a suspect in the death of a black inmate the last time he was imprisoned. The death was believed to have been motivated by a racial conflict between the Black Muslims and the White Aryan Race, of which Cedric was a proud member. No one bothered to investigate too hard, and no one was prosecuted.

We hummed along at seventy miles per hour for a few minutes until we topped a small rise and were suddenly confronted by the scene of an accident. A farmer on his tractor had been turning onto the highway from a dirt road when a pickup truck topped the hill a little too fast and crashed into it, overturning the tractor across the road and blocking both lanes. I slammed on the brakes and skidded toward the accident burning rubber. The cruiser fishtailed sideways, throwing up dirt and gravel from the shoulder. We finally came to a jarring halt just short of the overturned tractor.

Red and I had on our seatbelts, but Cedric crashed headfirst into the latticed steel dividers. When I turned to see how he was doing, blood was coming from a cut on his forehead, and he was crumpled forward letting out a series of low moans. Red got out of the car, opened the back door, and reached in, pulling Cedric up to a sitting position to see if he was hurt. I exited on the driver's side and, somewhat shaken, started around the car to assist Red.

What happened next occurred so fast it was hard to reconstruct the details. Cedric rushed Red, knocking him to the ground, and grabbed Red's gun from its holster. Then he swung toward me with the gun in his hand.

Without even thinking, I shot Cedric just below the waist. The big .45 slug broke his hipbone and sent him crashing to the ground. I ran to where he had fallen and stomped on his wrist with my cowboy-booted foot. I thought I felt Cedric's wrist break when he dropped Red's gun.

Red was writhing on the ground in apparent agony. His face was flushed, and he didn't seem to be able to breathe. Everything had happened so fast, I couldn't figure out how he'd been hurt. Just as I rushed to help him, he was able to roll onto his stomach. He let out strangled, wheezing cough, which dislodged the plug of tobacco from his throat, where it had been trapped, blocking his windpipe.

"Dirty bastard. I shouldn't have unlocked his cuffs," Red growled as he staggered to his feet.

"I'll call for an ambulance and help. Cedric's not going anywhere," I replied.

"Thanks for the help, Snake, but I wish you'd killed the son of a bitch. He sure would have killed us."

Cedric lay on the ground, seriously wounded, as I called for help on the car radio. The dispatcher said help was on the way. I got the first aid kit out of the car and stuffed a bandage into the wound in Cedric's hip, although the gaping hole spewing blood made it a little sick to look at. The recuffed Cedric still had the strength to snarl, "I'll get you, you dirty cocksucker," which reminded me of the joys of being in law enforcement.

Red went to see if anyone was hurt from the collision between the pickup and the tractor, soon reporting back that there seemed to be only minor injuries.

I'd never so much as pulled my gun on duty before, and the only thing I had ever shot at was a target. At first I felt all right, but after sitting down for a minute I got up and was hit by a wave of dizziness. It must have been shock. I sure as hell didn't want to kill anybody, even a violent piece of scum like Cedric. So I was relieved when an ambulance arrived with two paramedics who started a blood transfusion, used a pressure bandage to slow the bleeding, and loaded Cedric for a quick trip to the hospital in Clinton, about forty miles away. They said his wound was serious, but that he ought to survive.

Shortly the sheriff, another deputy, and a highway patrolman arrived. Red and I gave statements sitting in the highway patrol car. Then the patrolman and the sheriff interviewed the participants in the original wreck. Finally, after reconstructing the entire event half a dozen times, we loaded up and returned to town with me still driving and Red mumbling to himself about unlocking Cedric's cuffs.

CHAPTER 5

After the shooting I sat at my desk in the sheriff's office. The deputies all shared a bullpen, but each of us had our own desk and telephone. The furniture was a hodgepodge of ancient, grade-school wooden desks and standard-issue, metal government furniture.

I was leaning back in my not-too-uncomfortable chair with my feet on the desk, trying to make my mind go blank and simply forget the events of the day, when the phone rang.

"You okay, Snake? I just heard what happened." It was Judge Roberts, concerned about my well-being, as usual.

"I'm a little shaken up, Judge, but I'll be fine. I'm damn glad I didn't kill him."

"You're right. Even Cedric doesn't deserve to die. Although the county will be out a lot of money for medical care and another trial for assault and attempted escape. Hang in there, Partner. If you want to talk any time, drop by the office."

Judge Roberts was like an older brother, someone I'd looked up to from the time I was a kid, admiring his capacity for hard work and his stubborn commitment to the things in which he believed.

Don Ed grew up poor, and he was raised by his grandparents. His granddad worked as a janitor at my Dad's bank, and his grandmother cleaned houses and babysat with me to help make ends meet.

Don Ed loved the rodeo. He worked part-time on a ranch during high school so he could ride and rope. As soon as he graduated he hit the rodeo circuit, riding broncs and roping calves. He made just enough money to stay with it for a year or two, until he got stomped by a bucking horse at the night rodeo in Cody Wyoming and came home with a bad limp he'd have for the rest of his life. That's when he showed up in M.B.'s bank with no job and no collateral, asking for a loan to pay for his tuition and books at the state college over in Weatherford. M.B. loaned him the money and helped him find a part-time job. He didn't charge anything but interest on Don Ed's note while he barreled through college in three years with an almost perfect 4.0 average.

When Don Ed said he wanted to be a lawyer, and was going to night school in Oklahoma City, M.B. said fine and loaned him what he needed. Don Ed got a job as a law clerk in the public defender's office while he went to night law school, and unlike a lot of young lawyers who couldn't wait to graduate and make a big salary with some prestigious law firm, he stayed with the public defender when he finished school. That's where he was when he tried his first death penalty case, and he was hooked. All he wanted to do from then on was defend capital cases, and that's what he did—with an unrelenting tenacity that saved the lives of some really worthless individuals.

When he left the public defender's office and set up his own practice, most of his clients were bad to the bone and, like most criminals, poor. But he soon drew some cases involving celebrities. Don Ed fought just as hard for an indigent as he did for a millionaire, but he did, as he put it, "set aside a little for retirement" when he got the chance. He represented a Texas oilman who was charged with killing his wife. The evidence was circumstantial but seemingly overwhelming against the oilman, and the case was spread all over the national media. When Don Ed got the oilman off, his career as a private defense lawyer was made.

Later I asked Don Ed what he charged for the defense. He broke into a quizzical little smile and said, "They said he was a millionaire, so I charged him a million, cash, up front. After the trial he said it was the best damn deal he ever made. He was one of the few satisfied clients I ever had."

As soon as Don Ed could, he paid back all his loans at M.B.'s bank, but that wasn't the only thing that endeared him to my father. Don Ed was the example that M.B. used to motivate me, and because of my respect for Don Ed and my boyish impression of his rodeo prowess, it worked. I wanted to measure up to Don Ed's standards, and in some part I did.

At the same time Don Ed, out of gratitude to M.B., took on the task of watching out for me like a little brother. No easy task, given my native curiosity and my ingenuity in finding ways to learn about life. Remember, this was the age of "sex, drugs, and rock and roll," and they all appealed to me, although I quickly rejected the drug part after a limited experience smoking pot, unless you consider beer a drug.

In the end, it was Don Ed who helped me when I needed it most. When I was out of work, divorced, and grieving over M.B.'s fate, it was Don Ed who got me a job as a deputy sheriff and process server. That job led to work checking mineral titles for bankruptcy trustees who took control of many of the go-go oil companies of the seventies and early eighties that were gone by the nineties. Simply stated, Don Ed was my mentor and my best friend.

No sooner had Don Ed hung up than the phone rang again. "Hey, Dirty Harry, you're still goin' to play ball tonight, aren't you?" It was Mad Mike, reminding me this was our night for full-contact basketball with the coaches at Southwestern State College in Weatherford.

"I don't feel so great, Mike, but maybe it will take my mind off this shooting."

"Hell, in Vietnam I saw more blood than that before breakfast. I just hope it doesn't affect your jump shot—it's bad enough already. I'll see you at seven tonight."

Mike was a wildly enthusiastic, totally out of control basketball player. He would put up shots from anywhere and make more than you might expect. As far as any teamwork was concerned, forget it. His whole concept of the game was to get his hands on the ball and let fly. The other players all called him "Gunner" with good cause.

A few had even suggested he not show up, but Mike loved to play, ignored any criticism, and went right on playing his own game. His hero was Woody Harrelson, partly because of Woody's basketball movie, but mostly because of Woody's outspoken advocacy of hemp, which was close enough to one of Mike's staple items.

My basketball shoes and shorts were in my car, so I drove straight to Weatherford, about thirty miles away. In western Oklahoma distances are such that thirty miles is right around the corner.

When I arrived the rest of our "team" was already warming up on the court. Mike, dressed in a Grateful Dead T-shirt, soiled and worn gray gym shorts, black socks, and black, high-top basketball shoes, was practicing long jump shots. Our other guard, Alonzo Two Bears, was near the basket, rebounding and tipping balls to the shooters. Alonzo was fast, he had a nice touch, and he was a good ball handler. He had one small problem—he was almost legally blind. It was always best to yell "Alonzo" when you threw him a pass so he would look in the right direction. The rest of the team was composed of another deputy sheriff and a tall, skinny, somewhat uncoordinated teaching assistant.

The coaches were pretty much standard-issue, small-college jocks—way too serious—and that was our advantage. We could always get under their skin. Especially Mike, who talked an unrelenting line of trash.

The game started and quickly degenerated into the usual chaotic run and shoot that characterizes thousands of similar pickup games all over the country. This night, Mike happened to be hitting, Alonzo was quick on the fast break, and I handled the assistant defensive football coach inside, in spite of the vicious elbows he threw in my direction. To the disgust of the coaches, we eked out a victory.

Mike and I went to T-Bone's for a beer. Mike's conversation was always the same after a game. He replayed the whole thing, describing his own performance in Jordanesque terms. When we won, it was because of his heroic play. When we lost, it was a result of the ineptitude of his teammates. The more beer he drank, the better he played. I felt better listening to Mike, drinking beer, and forgetting about Cedric.

Mike was a lot more interested in basketball than in his love life. When I brought up Sally he said he was glad she was gone. The idea that Freight Train might show up any time made him nervous. When he was nervous he smoked too much pot, and then he couldn't fly. No flying meant less income, which made him fall behind in his alimony and child support payments to his first three wives. The mention of pot made Mike remember it was time for a joint, so he decided to leave and head home. I was suddenly exhausted and ready to crash myself.

Leaving T-Bone's, I started across the darkened parking lot for my car, fumbling in my pocket for my keys. As I reached my car, a large, shadowy figure stepped out from behind the car parked next to mine.

I recognized the man known as General Sherman from Morford's court hearing. Still dressed in military clothes, the general said in a deep, powerful voice, "Don't be alarmed, Deputy, I mean you no harm." He stepped toward me in an intimidating manner, making the hair rise on the back of my neck. There was something about Sherman that was inherently menacing. He could have been comic in his appearance, but there was nothing funny about him, and his entire persona presented a deadly serious threat.

"What do you want?"

"I need your services," the general responded.

"Call me at the office. I'll be in tomorrow."

"This is not office business. It concerns government oppression. I hear you know how to use a gun. We need good men who believe in patriotism and will fight for liberty. Morford says you come from good stock and understand how the Constitution has been violated by our government. I'm sure being a deputy sheriff you are aware of the degeneration of government and the corruption of the heritage of freemen."

"I'm tired, Mr. Sherman. I had to shoot a man today, and I have no interest in you or your cause. Don't contact me again."

"Think about it," Sherman said as he disappeared back into the dark.

Driving home, I thought about the intensity of Sherman's voice, his hard, pig eyes, and his apparent commitment to his cause. There was something in him that engendered in me a primal feeling of readiness. He reeked of pent-up violence and raised my every defense against what seemed cold and inhumane—more than evil. He was, without doubt, formidable and dangerous.

CHAPTER 6

Several weeks passed and I forgot about the general and Morford and, except for an occasional bad night, Cedric as well. I served legal papers and spent a lot of time in Arapahoe, the county seat of Custer County, checking title on oil and gas interests owned by a now-bankrupt oil company.

Checking the title to minerals is a time-consuming and laborious task. It requires concentration to avoid overlooking a transaction that may affect the ownership of the mineral interests under a particular tract.

Land has been divided by U.S. Government Survey into units known as townships. Townships are identified by range, which indicates the distance from the nearest government-surveyed north–south meridian line. Each township is six miles by six miles in area, containing thirty-six sections which are each one square mile or six hundred and forty acres. The sections are then frequently divided into quarters or portions of quarters. Thus minerals may be leased by descriptions, such as NW/4 of the SE/4 of Section 2, Township 21, Range 30 I.M. (Indian Meridian), indicating the location of a forty-acre tract.

As years pass, the surface may rarely change hands, but the minerals may be leased, sold, assigned, mortgaged, conveyed by a will through probate proceedings, executed on to satisfy a court judgment, or effected by other legal instruments referring to particular interests. This may result in the mineral ownership being broken up into small fractions that have to be expressed in tiny percentages.

An index of the documents filed with the county clerk is kept by hand entry in large, ponderous index books which weigh ten or twelve pounds each. The actual document filed is recorded, copied, returned to the appropriate party, and then referred to by book and page numbers in order of filing by time and date. Thus, a lease might be filed at book one hundred, page three of the county clerk's records.

When an oil company establishes that an area is a good prospect for drilling, the company must then determine who owns or has the right to drill under the prospective area. Then, either a lease can be obtained from the owner or an assignment from the lessee, if the minerals are already under lease.

To ascertain the ownership, a title check or "take off" from the records is needed. As a landman, this was sometimes part of my job. I could spend hours standing, or occasionally sitting, pouring through index books and old records to supply the company with the information they needed. Rather than finding this boring, I enjoyed the calm, quiet, intellectual break from my duties as a deputy sheriff and my work as a process server, which entailed dealing with people, many of them hostile and some criminal.

My work for oil companies also included obtaining oil and gas leases from mineral owners. The company would furnish me with a printed or typed lease and a bank draft. The lease offered a bonus in cash for signing and a percentage interest in the proceeds of oil and gas sold from the property. The terms varied based on the projected production of wells to be drilled on the property, although there were some fairly standard rules of thumb, the royalty or percentage interest currently being a three-sixteenth.

Since I was a local boy and many of the mineral owners I dealt with knew either M.B. or me personally, or by reputation, I had good results obtaining leases and got a fair amount of work from oil companies, particularly the small independents that didn't employ landmen full-time but used contract workers like myself. I was paid a day rate plus expenses, and the work was profitable.

As a process server, I served summons on defendants in civil cases or subpoenas for witnesses, ordering their appearance in all manner of legal actions, both civil and criminal. Although some of the served individuals took the service with resignation, others were verbally abusive or even physically hostile. Over the years I grew tired of this work, which didn't pay very well, and tried to spend more and more time as a landman, which paid better and was vastly more interesting and rewarding.

Following my usual routine, I was up early, worked hard all day, and then ran five miles. The work, the running, and the mindless routine kept me sane. It gave me a rhythm for my life. Sometimes I missed the highs and lows, but they always came whether you planned them or not, so the calm periods in between had to be accepted and, to the extent possible, enjoyed.

I rented a small, wooden-frame house just outside of town. It was located on a two-lane blacktop road that ran along a section line stretching to a busier county road a few miles away. The house was quiet and isolated from any neighbors. It gave me privacy and, although somewhat dilapidated, I liked its location. No phone, no pool, no pets, no roommate, and a good place to run. My landlord even mowed the yard. What else could a person really need?

The running was my escape from reality. It kept my mind off of more serious subjects. My usual route was mostly flat, and since nearly the whole county is flat, that wasn't unusual. I liked to run in the evenings a little before dusk. The mornings were cooler in the summer, but the evening runs suited my habits. Probably the best thing about western Oklahoma is the lack of people. There is plenty of open space, and I liked being in it—without the urban rush of San Francisco. Running into what seemed like endless space, disappearing into endless time, often suited my mood and calmed me in a way almost nothing else could. It was also a way to help me try to keep my weight under two hundred pounds, a benchmark I had trouble making.

After I ran I would stretch, put on an old sweatshirt, and open a beer. Beer was my drug of choice. I didn't like whiskey, and wine didn't go well with chicken fried steak and country gravy—the haute cuisine of western Oklahoma—or the minimalist meals I cooked for myself on most nights. Then I would read, often for hours. I only watched news and sports on TV, and I wasn't usually interested in the movies that came to our one theater, so my life was reading. I read fiction, non-fiction—everything from *Sports Illustrated*, to the classics, to mystery novels. Reading was my yacht and my private golf course. As far as I know, it did me no particular good, except to provide me with huge amounts of trivia that interested almost no one else. But to me, it was more than a habit or a diversion—it was part of life.

Then there were the birds. I didn't have any pets. After Kit, I didn't want any kind of permanent relationship, even with an animal, but I loved birds. There was a feeder hanging on a tree right outside my kitchen window. Most of the birds that came were sparrows or starlings, but I also had blue jays, robins, mocking birds, pigeons, doves, cardinals, and a few times even a hummingbird. I loved to watch the birds at my house and along the roads and in the fields. Hawks and turkey buzzards could be seen in the skies along with migrating ducks and geese. Doves, scissortail flycatchers, and swallows perched on the high lines. Sometimes you could see quail or prairie hens along the road. Whatever my mood, watching birds always made me feel better. I even looked forward to hearing their chirping in the morning just before my alarm clock went off, signaling the beginning of the day.

Some people might call my life lonely. I would describe it as solitary. Living alone isn't necessarily lonely. What is really lonely is living with someone you don't want to be with and not figuring out a way to leave.

When I did start to feel lonely or depressed, or think too much about myself, I would write. I don't know what inspired me or even when exactly I began to write, but for a long time I was a closet poet and songwriter. The writing was for my own amusement. However, recently I had gotten up the nerve to show some of my work to Mike,

Don Ed, or Red. Writing was fun, and it kept me from dwelling on more serious thoughts. A poem my friends seemed to like was "Hattie the One-Legged Whore."

THE BALLAD OF HATTIE, THE ONE-LEGGED WHORE

Hattie went to whorin'
when her husband up and died
and she couldn't live on promises
or the gold he couldn't find

She said she'd make a living
and was not about to beg
It didn't seem to matter
that she only had one leg

She didn't want no charity
or complain about bad luck
she figured she could make it
just as long as she could fuck

In fact she used her handicap
to advertise her trade
and she was quite successful
when it came to getting laid

The cowhands they all liked her
'cause she didn't waste their pay
but she really had them do it
in a most peculiar way

She'd have that cowboy
climb aboard while she was standing up
then she'd drop her wooden leg
and she'd begin to buck

Hattie'd go to hoppin'
just to keep a standin' up
and the cowboy had to ride her
or he couldn't saddle up

It's said a ride on Hattie
beat any bronc around
'cause she knew just how to do it
so no cowboy hit the ground

So I guess there's a moral
to this tale you thought was crap
and the moral to the story
is to hire the handicapped

People asked me where in the world I got the idea for the poem. It came from a story out of Steinbeck's *The Grapes of Wrath*. You can check it out.

CHAPTER 7

Sometimes I would think about how I managed to find myself back in Cordell. Like everything in life, it was a matter of timing.

After college I took a job in San Francisco with Bank of America. After sending me through an executive training program, I was assigned to a job as a loan officer dealing with start-up companies, mostly in the high tech field. My customers prospered, made money, borrowed more money, and paid their debts. Through little of my own doing, I became a rising star in the commercial lending department and began to advance with the bank. Advancement meant better pay and even an expense account. I rented a fancy apartment on Russian Hill and bought a new Porsche. I had season tickets for the 49ers and the Giants and played basketball at the Olympic Club.

Life was going great and seemed even better when I met Kit. She was perfect, or so I thought. I can't be sure I was ever in love with Kit. I do know I was totally infatuated by her, and I was something, not necessarily someone, she needed—or at least could use at the time. If love means forgiving the unforgivable, then she was never in love with me, but that's not how it started.

A college friend invited me to a party at his house in Sausalito. There were too many people, it was too loud, and after ten minutes I wasn't sure why I'd showed up at all. I was about to leave when I saw Kit. She was stylishly dressed in a tight, black dress and black high heels. She had cold, black hair cut short in a severe style. Tall and slender—to me she was beautiful.

The host introduced me as a former football star at Stanford.

Her response with a sardonic smile was, "How droll."

"I take it you're not a sports fan. What do you like to do?" I replied.

"That's not much of a line, but I like fencing and yoga."

"We don't do a lot of that in Oklahoma. When we say fencing we mean building fence."

"I've never been to Oklahoma. Is it nice?"

"I'm not sure nice is the right word, but I like it."

"So you're a cowboy?"

"Not exactly, ma'am, just a humble banker."

"There are no humble bankers. I hate bankers, but not as much as I hate this party. Let's go someplace outside."

So we did. We left the party and went to the Alta Mira Hotel to sit on the deck overlooking the Bay and listen to a corny combo playing outdated show tunes at a wedding reception in the ballroom. Kit was a psychologist, a PhD graduate of California Berkeley, who practiced in San Francisco. Her face, for lack of a better term, was exotic. I was fascinated by her. She was bright, beautiful, and different from any woman I had ever known. Luckily, she found me funny. She got a great laugh out of calling me Snake and, once knowing the nickname, never addressed me any other way.

About midnight I took her back to get her car at the party. Before I could ask for her telephone number, she leaned over and kissed me. I tried to return the kiss, but she was already out of the car.

"How about going sailing Saturday? Meet me at the Embarcadero Ferry at nine o'clock, and don't be late, Mr. Snake."

The fact that I knew nothing about sailing didn't stop me from showing up, and there she was dressed in jeans, a sweatshirt, and tennis shoes. I had worn what I thought was a sailing costume, which happened to be the same outfit. We took the ferry to Sausalito and, along with two of Kit's friends, spent the day sailing on the San Francisco Bay.

We rode the ferry back to San Francisco just at dusk. The lights were coming on across the city, and as much as I liked the sight, I couldn't take my eyes off of Kit.

When we docked she looked at me and said, "Snake, you were a good sport for someone who didn't know a thing about sailing. You qualify to take me to dinner."

"What if I'm busy?"

"Your loss. See you at Buena Vista at eight. Oh, unless you're busy."

Of course I was there, and again and again as long as she kept asking. She always dictated when we would meet and never let me initiate any of our plans. I met her with greater and greater frequency and our good-byes grew longer, until one night she asked me to follow her home. We went to her apartment in a converted Victorian house in the Haight. Her room was lit by candlelight and her body smelled of some type of incense she burned for effect. We made love for the first time on her couch. She was passionate and aggressive. She took control over my body, and I gladly relinquished myself to her until we were both satisfied. I spent the night and most nights from then on.

We both worked hard all day, and her practice was busy and successful. After several months we were standing at the sink in her kitchen, and she turned to me and said, "Do snakes have babies or eggs?"

"Is there something you're trying to tell me?"

"I'm not pregnant, but I want to have a child."

"Well I may not be all that smart, but I am strong and healthy. Maybe I could be the father."

"What does that mean, Snake?"

"Let's get married."

"That's a big decision. I'd think about it some more, but I already have. I accept."

"When?" I responded.

"How about two weeks from Saturday. Call M.B. and I'll call my parents. I've already called the Alta Mira. We can do it there."

"What if I'd said no?"

"Your loss, cowboy."

The wedding was at the Alta Mira overlooking San Francisco Bay on a sunny, pristine, fall afternoon. The sun sparkled off the bay and Kit looked beautiful in a short, stylish white dress. Kit organized it and there were over a hundred people, nearly all her friends, and most importantly, doctors and others who could help in her practice.

M.B. made it and was my best man. Don Ed was tied up in a big trial and couldn't come, but did call and send a humorous telegram. A few people came at my invitation, friends from the bank and college. M.B. was polite and reserved, as always. I could tell he had some reservations about Kit, but in his usual fashion said nothing, wished her good luck, and gave me a handsome check as a wedding gift. He was happy I had found a wife and I think may have even looked forward to the prospect of a grandchild.

That's how I happened to have a wife. But not for long.

CHAPTER 8

After Kit and I married, she insisted I move into her apartment. It was inconvenient, but I didn't really mind. She still arranged and scheduled all of our activities. Our social life was based on her contacts and friends, cultivated largely to enhance her growing psychological practice.

During this time, I was following what was happening in Oklahoma but was busy with my own job, so only superficially. In the late seventies and early eighties, the economy in western Oklahoma exploded. A gold rush mentality prevailed as paper millionaires raced each other to lease oil and gas interests and sought to tap an ocean of natural gas trapped deep beneath the surface in a geological area known as the Anadarko Basin. Clever promoters roamed the world, inducing doctors, lawyers, Wall Street brokers, and other investors to sink their money into oil and gas wells, which drilled deeper and deeper beneath the red clay of western Oklahoma.

For a time it seemed as though everyone was rich. The cost of oil field services skyrocketed, and farmers sold oil and gas leases for more than the value of their entire farms. Motels and restaurants sprung up in towns that could scarcely support a small grocery store before the boom.

Not only could these instant millionaires raise funds, they could spend them even faster. One oil man with little more than a grade school education and the guts to ask investors for big numbers owned a yacht, a jet plane, a cigarette boat, and bought all of his employees Mercedes to drive as company cars. This new breed of wildcatters threw legendary parties—champagne, cocaine, and good-looking women seemed to be available twenty-four hours a day. A previously little-known drilling contractor from Woodward spent $500,000 on his daughter's wedding. It was a game of "can you top this" played with private helicopters, huge mansions, jewelry, and every kind of expensive adult toy available.

Everyone was suddenly an oilman. Salesmen, teachers, football coaches, doctors, lawyers, and others with no training, experience, or background rushed into the oil business. They even seemed to adopt a uniform—an open-necked shirt with too much gold jewelry and cowboy boots. They filled the bars and expensive restaurants and talked constantly in the jargon of the business about huge oil deals, armed with only the thinnest knowledge of the subject they discussed. It was a big liar's picnic.

Even some experienced oil and gas professionals were caught up in the frenzy and overextended their credit to drill prospects they otherwise would have never touched. The price of oil was predicted to rise to sixty dollars a barrel and actually did hit forty, but like all commodities, the market adjusted and the price went down as fast as it had gone up, falling all the way to eight dollars.

Looking back, it was clearly a blueprint for disaster, and when the bubble burst, all the paper millionaires went down faster than the price of oil. Unfortunately, they took the whole state with them. When the high rollers failed, so did a lot of the hard working people who made a living working for, or selling goods and services to, the oil companies. Even worse off were the banks that had recklessly extended credit with little or no real security for their loans.

The root source of the whole wild trip was banks. Bankers proved to be the dumbest businessmen of all. They loaned money to people with no credit, no oil and gas experience, and little more than a vague idea of where they were going to drill. One oil company went bankrupt, and when the trustee appointed by the court arrived to examine the corporate records, all he could find was a jumble of unrelated papers stuffed in shoeboxes. Interest rates and inflation soared as the bankers shoveled money out the door into the hands of charlatans, who spent most of it on their own personal lifestyles. The bankers simply lost their heads. That is, most bankers. Duane Lucas stayed calm and calculating. He waited with the patience of a cobra for others to fail, and he was not disappointed.

On July 4, 1982, Penn Square Bank in Oklahoma City collapsed. This small, shopping center bank was the catalyst for the money that financed the oil boom. Incredibly, Penn Square had been able to influence Continental Bank of Chicago, Seafirst of Seattle, Michigan National Bank, and other major banks across the country to participate in loans originated by Penn Square. Penn Square's go-go bank officers scoffed at prudent banking procedures, not even properly documenting loans. The Penn Square vice president in charge of oil and gas lending drank whiskey from a cowboy boot and danced on tables at a local nightspot. He memorialized multi-million dollar loans with handwritten notes scratched on stationary and stuffed into his desk drawer. In spite of these practices, the bank loaned out billions of dollars—far beyond its own lending limits—by passing huge balances on to the bigger banks, who joined in the frenzy of the exploding oil and gas business.

When Penn Square failed and was closed by the FDIC, it set off a chain reaction that brought down a large part of the U.S. banking industry, with bigger and bigger banks falling like a house of cards. Unfortunately, it also brought down almost every bank in Oklahoma.

CHAPTER 9

While I knew about Penn Square's failure, I couldn't believe it would have any effect on Cordell National because of its small size and M.B.'s conservative management. That is, until I got a call from Don Ed at work. My secretary, duly impressed, advised me that "Judge Roberts is calling."

"Don Ed, to what do I owe this honor, Your Honor?"

"Snake, I'm worried about M.B. I'm sure he's too proud to have told you, but I understand the bank is in financial trouble. He looks terrible. You need to get back here and see if you can give him some help. I'm no banker, but you can't believe what's going on in this state. The biggest and richest people are going bankrupt, banks and savings and loans are closing, the price of oil has gone to hell, and the whole place is in the crapper."

"You're right about M.B. He would never tell me anything about trouble. A phone call is no good, so I guess I'll be seeing you soon. Thanks as always, Don Ed."

"Drop by when you get to town. I'll see if I can pick up any more information on the bank. You know how lawyers like to talk, but what you don't know is most of us are damn good listeners. I'll see what I can hear around town."

I told my boss I had to take a few days off for family business and then called Kit. Her secretary said she was in a conference with a patient and would call me back, and in a few minutes she did.

"What's up, Snake? You never call me at the office."

"Don Ed called. He says M.B.'s in financial trouble and he's worried about him. I have to go home and see if I can help. I'm leaving tomorrow morning."

"Well, I hope you don't miss that party for the museum on Saturday. It's important that I be there. Dr. Wright's wife is in charge, and he refers me a lot of patients."

"You may have to go without me, but I'm sure I'll be back right away." A prediction that soon proved false.

I called M.B. and asked him to meet me at the Oklahoma City Airport. He sounded tired and was surprised I was coming home. I didn't question him about the bank over the phone, as I knew he would deny any trouble. M.B. believed everybody should take care of their own problems, and that a person's difficulties were no one else's business. He hated to ask anyone for help. If he ever had a problem, he would take care of it himself, in his own way.

M.B. met me at the Airport in Oklahoma City, and I was startled by his appearance. He had lost weight from his already lean frame and looked ten years older. We started for Cordell, some two hours distant. M.B. always drove big, substantial cars, and his current one was no exception—a Lincoln Town Car—although I did notice it was three or four years old. Like everyone in western Oklahoma, M.B. drove fast. Our part of the state is big and wide open, and people routinely cover long miles between small towns over distances that might seem extreme in a more urban setting.

Once M.B. hit the interstate, he put the car on cruise control at eighty and settled in for the trip to Clinton, where we turned off to head down a two-lane road, south, into Cordell.

"It's good to see you, Son, but to what do I owe this pleasure? You never come home since you got married."

"No use bullshitting, Dad. You always taught me to get right down to business and talk straight."

"I'm glad at least a little bit of what I taught you took."

"I hear the bank has financial problems, and I want to know if that's true, and if there's anything I can do to help."

"That's two questions. So I'll answer them one at a time. The bank examiners have us under scrutiny. I'm arguing with them over whether we have sufficient capital to stay in business, and whether we should write off some of our loans. I think we can survive, but it's close. The bank really needs more capital. That's the answer to your first question. As to your second one, I don't see how you can help, unless you've saved up a lot of money fast."

"Thanks for telling me what's happening. I know it must be serious for you to admit there's a problem. Maybe just talking to me about it will help. I might have some ideas. You know, I'm a banker, too."

"Yes and I'm proud of what you've done, but I don't think you've got any assets to contribute to capital."

"Not unless you count a Porsche with a big loan on it, but I may have some ideas. How much capital do you need?"

"I'd say fifteen million was enough, but twenty would be better." I must have looked as stunned as I felt, because M.B. let out a little chuckle and continued. "You asked me to talk straight, and there's no use being anything but candid. I run the bank, I'm responsible for the problem, and I'll take care of it."

"What about your farm? It's got to be worth close to a million at today's prices. Why don't you mortgage that and put the money into the bank? Then there are all those stocks you own and your retirement account—that must be another million at least."

"I have already put everything I own into the bank. I sold the farm and all of my stocks and contributed the proceeds to capital. We're still short at least fifteen million dollars."

"Call Mr. Vose at the First National in Oklahoma City. You've always been on good terms and have done business with him over the years."

"You won't believe this, but the First is in trouble. It may fail."

"That's impossible. That bank has been around since statehood. It's the biggest in the state and solid as a rock."

"That's what a lot of people thought, but this whole deal is crazy.

Almost every bank in the state has either been closed by the FDIC or is under supervision and scrambling for existence."

"Well, Dad, we can't give up. I have banking connections all over the country through Bank of America. Let's go to work."

When we got to Cordell, we went right to the bank. M.B. gave me the most recent financial statements and the files on the loans the examiners wanted written off. I went into the bank's conference room and closed the door. Five hours later M.B. came in and asked me to come to dinner. We talked some more, and I went back to work until I fell asleep in my chair and had to have the night security guard let me out to walk home.

CHAPTER 10

After a brief and fitful night's sleep, I returned to the bank to continue studying the records. The day passed quickly as I concentrated on digesting the bank's financial information. The loan portfolios read like a bad horror story. Loans that were secured by what appeared to be good collateral began to disintegrate as the price of oil, and then farm and ranch land, fell precipitously. The borrower's cash flow plummeted, and they could not repay their debts. The bank moved more money from capital into reserves for bad debts, and the problems compounded, draining the bank's capital account and driving it below the minimum amount required by law.

Even though the situation looked bad, it appeared there was hope. What goes down must come up at some point, and a recovery in the price of oil or a good wheat crop could go a long way toward pulling the bank out, if we could just hang on long enough.

On the good side, M.B. had not loaned any money to fly-by-night promoters or wannabe oilmen. The borrowers were experienced, independent oil and gas producers, drilling contractors, oil field service companies, and farmers who simply had been wracked by the devastating oil and gas and agricultural markets. M.B.'s injections of capital had also somewhat righted the situation.

When I had finished reviewing most of the bad loans, M.B. and I met and mapped out a plan to try and save the bank. M.B. would stay in the bank and try to deal with the examiners and work on collecting the bad loans. I would go to Bank of America and any other banking connections I had to try to raise capital or, as a last resort, sell the bank. Although he wouldn't admit it, M.B. was clearly glad to have my help and even seemed to stand up a little straighter when I left his office to start arranging meetings all over the country.

I called my boss at Bank of America and told him I had to use all of my vacation and sick leave, and then take a leave of absence, if necessary. He wasn't happy, but after he understood the situation, he wished me luck, and referred me to a vice president in the department that dealt with corresponding banks. The vice president was willing to arrange for an appointment, which, unfortunately, later proved to be fruitless.

Then I called Kit and told her I would be home briefly and then gone for at least a few weeks. She was peeved and asked me to finish my business as soon as possible. I assured her I would be home as soon as I found new financing for the bank.

My life quickly transcended into a maelstrom of work. For six months I was either on the phone or in an airplane. I chased down possible leads from bankers to financiers, bogus entrepreneurs, junk dealers, and bottom feeders, crisscrossing the county and meeting with everyone who might possibly invest in the bank. I ate poorly and slept mainly on airplanes and in airports. At least twice I was sure I had made a deal to raise money for the bank, only to see the transaction fall apart at the last minute. I even flew to the Cayman Islands, where a very proper British solicitor introduced me to his client, a "businessman" from Columbia who clearly wanted a way to launder drug money in the United States.

Occasionally I returned to Cordell to discuss matters with M.B. Each time I grew increasingly alarmed at his appearance and the news he gave me about the bank's financial status. These meetings just motivated me more to find a solution to our problems. I became obsessed with obtaining a financial remedy for the bank and was totally preoccupied with my goal and had no time for anything else, including Kit. I saw her once for a few hours when I was in San Francisco talking to a venture capital firm, and I called her occasionally from airports or motels. At first she was irritated by my absence, then angry, and then finally cold. Her voice grew flat, calm, and devoid of all emotion. It must have been the tone she used with her mentally disturbed patients, to try to bring them back to reality without reacting to their fears or ravings. When this happened, I would lose my temper and our conversations would quickly degenerate into arguments, followed by my contrite expressions of love, which seemed unable to penetrate her carefully practiced, calm veneer.

Then one night I called her from the Cleveland airport. She had been letting many of my calls go to her answering machine, but she took this one. After telling her where I was, I inquired about how she was doing.

"Snake, I didn't marry someone to be by myself. I thought we agreed to have a child. If you are not back here for good by the weekend, don't come back at all."

In my already disturbed state, this was more than I could take. I came unraveled and attacked her as a selfish, cold-hearted bitch. Before I could finish, she hung up the phone. On the plane to Dallas, I began to calm down and, of course, felt terrible about what I had said. As soon as I was on the ground, I tried to call her to apologize, but all I got was her answering machine, and that's all I got from then on, whether I called her at home or the office.

As bad as I felt about Kit, I put my feelings aside to work on my job of saving the bank. I thought things could be patched up with her after I accomplished what had become my all-consuming purpose in life, and once more plunged into another series of endless meetings and presentations.

Finally, after about six months, I returned to Cordell to meet with M.B. Somehow driving from the Oklahoma City airport to the bank, I had a strange and empty feeling. Call it a premonition, or maybe just a reflection of the reality of the situation, but it was there in my stomach like a bowl of bad chili. When I got to the bank, M.B. told me to come into his office immediately. He looked even worse than the last time I had seen him. His complexion had a sickly, gray-green cast, and although he still stood ramrod straight, I could tell things were bad.

M.B. sat down behind his desk and assumed the posture he always took when he was going to lecture me about something.

"Son, I appreciate everything you've done to help, but I have taken care of the problem myself. I caused it and I've solved it. I sold the bank and we have to get out by five o'clock today so the new owner can take over tomorrow when business opens."

"Dad, we can still make it. I talked to a guy in Dallas who represents some Saudi's with plenty of money. I've already got a ticket to Cyprus to meet them. Don't give up now."

"It's too late. The examiners were going to close the bank tomorrow. I couldn't let that happen."

"But who in the hell would buy this bank, and what would they pay for it in this condition?"

M.B. got a little smile on his face and responded, "That's two questions. I'll answer them one at a time. The price was one dollar and an agreement to put in enough capital to save the bank. I owe that to all of my depositors. They're all friends and neighbors who have trusted me all their lives.

He paused and then said, "The buyer was Duane Lucas."

"Dad, you can't sell to that sorry son of a bitch. I don't believe it. Why would he want the bank?"

"He stole it. You and I know those properties that secure our loans will come back. Lucas can wait out the economy or, better yet, foreclose and suck up more oil and gas and real estate interests. He'll be even richer than he is now, but at least in the meantime nobody who has deposited money in the bank will be hurt.

"But, Dad, they're insured up to $100,000 anyway. Let it go. You don't have to deal with Lucas."

"I already have. Clear out your desk. I'm going home at five o'clock and so are you. At least you can get back to your wife."

So that was it. We failed. M.B. and I couldn't save the bank. I went to my office and sat there looking out the window at the courthouse thinking about nothing, just sitting and looking at the dust blowing across the square, pushed along by the everlasting

Oklahoma wind. I sat there for a long time until I saw Red come out of the courthouse carrying some papers. He walked across the street to the bank and came inside. Then there was a knock on my door.

"Snake, it's me, Red. I hate to do this, but I got divorce papers here from California. I got to serve them on you."

"It's okay, Red. Throw them on the desk. I can't get any lower."

I felt more numb than depressed. I didn't get drunk. I'd tried that before when I wanted to forget something, and all it did was give me a hangover and make me feel worse. For me, drinking was for celebrations and happy times.

If M.B. had the guts to give up everything he owned to a man he despised in order to save his friends and his reputation, I figured I could sure take care of my own problems with Kit. I called her again and got her answering machine. Then I booked a ticket for San Francisco and took off to get a plane out of Oklahoma City.

Arriving in San Francisco in the evening, I took a cab to our apartment. Parking in San Francisco is a nightmare, and we only had a one-car garage. Naturally, Kit used the garage. My car was kept in a public garage several blocks away which charged a ridiculous price for a parking space. When I reached the door of our second-floor apartment, I found the lock had already been changed. I knocked and rang the bell, but Kit wasn't home.

Descending the stairs, I saw Kit and a man I'd never seen before standing on the street next to a car embracing and kissing. They broke apart and Kit turned to walk to the building as the man drove away.

"Remember me? I'm the guy you used to know."

Kit never lost her composure but only said, "Snake, you made your choice. You are not welcome here. Talk to my lawyer. He'll make arrangements for you to get your things out of the apartment."

"I don't even rate an old-fashioned go to hell or a good-bye kiss?"

"If you don't leave me alone, I'll call the police."

"Give me a fuckin' break. I'm here to talk to you about our marriage."

"I told you, it's too late. Good-bye." She turned and entered the building without the slightest indication of any emotion at all, and I haven't seen her since.

Once my car was packed, I headed back to Cordell. It didn't seem like there was any reason to stay in San Francisco. Working in a bank was the last thing I wanted to do after my experiences with Cordell National. So I was headed back to Oklahoma like some old dust bowl Okie whose luck had played out in the land of golden opportunity. I was reminded of the old Woody Guthrie song that offered failure in California if "you ain't got the do-re-me." At least I was driving a Porsche and not a broken-down truck with a mattress tied to the roof.

On the way home I detoured to the Grand Canyon. I'd never seen the Canyon before, and just looking at it made me feel better. It was bigger and more impressive than photographs could portray. The millions of years of geological history were layered in the many colors created by nature. Every shade of orange, gray, purple, and brown contrasted with the green of the trees along the rim and scattered throughout the canyon. The sun reflected off of the angles of the rock outcroppings and created highlights and shadows based on the depth and angle of the rocks. I saw what the Indians first saw and what had captivated the generations that followed from John Wesley Powell to the present. As usual, the forces of nature vastly exceeded anything man could create or even imagine.

I decided to climb down and camp in the canyon. Climbing into and out of the Grand Canyon is a unique experience. It's the reverse of most hard climbs since you go downhill first and then have to climb back up to the rim of the canyon, making the second half of the climb the more strenuous. I went down the Kaibob Trail, which is steeper but shorter than some of the other trails. Going down is a lot faster, but still eight or nine miles of descent. Your quadriceps generally turn either to jelly or, in my case, concrete.

Coming out, I chose the Bright Angel Trail. A little longer than, but not quite as steep as, the Kaibob—thank God. It was plenty steep enough for a flatlander. Like most hard climbs, the steepest part is at the top, and the last long series of switchbacks seemed to take forever. At least it was in the fall, avoiding the almost unbelievable summer heat. I was totally exhausted by the time I reached the canyon's rim, but elated by my achievement of climbing up and down a total of 9,000 vertical feet and less obsessed over the loss of Kit.

The climb helped me clear my head and realize I was fed up with the greedy, materialistic yuppies of California. Surely the yuppies are the one of the worst classes of people in the history of the United States. The beatniks were existentialist, and to some extent antisocial, but did not try to force themselves or their beliefs onto anyone. The hippies advocated peace and love, and what could really be wrong with that philosophy? They may have been a little dirty and smoked a lot of dope but, in retrospect, had small impact on society in general. On the other hand, the dreaded yuppies have driven the country toward a materialistic society where success is measured by the number of expensive items a person can acquire. They are selfish, greedy, and devoid of almost any redeeming virtue. How barren a life must be that is measured solely by financial and social success. And what message does that send to their one-and-a-half perfect children, who are forced into soccer leagues, tennis lessons, and expensive private schools where educational systems turn out little cookie-cutter people and censor, rather than promote, the expansion of ideas and thoughts?

In a way, maybe the failure of M.B.'s bank was a lucky event. It made me realize that money was certainly not the end goal of life and realize, through the actions of my father, what real character meant. Maybe it was his background based in the fervent patriotism of WWII and his military service, but for whatever cause, he had a code of honor and a way of life that set him apart from the moneygrubbing, self-centered, "upwardly mobile" people who had been part of my life in San Francisco. Better yet, it saved me from continuing down that path myself, without even being conscious of my own direction. All of these thoughts came easier as

I traveled back to a new beginning—not knowing my future, but not regretting my past.

After a hot shower, a few beers, a steak, and a good night's sleep in Flagstaff, I decided to drive straight through to Cordell. I headed east on Interstate 40 at a steady eighty-five miles an hour listening to a little traveling music—Steve Earle's "Guitar Town."

East of Albuquerque the highway gets flat and the terrain is boring—nothing but miles and miles of nothing but miles and miles. Somewhere near Amarillo, I made up my mind to stay in Cordell. There was nothing left for me in San Francisco, and M. B.'s health looked bad. He was all the family I had, and I figured maybe I could help him get started again and do the same thing for myself.

CHAPTER 11

When I got home, I had to find a job. The person I turned to was Don Ed, and he came through, as usual. He got Sheriff Checker to hire me part-time as a deputy and used his considerable influence to persuade most of the lawyers in his judicial district to use me as a process server. Later I began to pick up work checking land titles for the bankruptcy court in Oklahoma City and finally, when the oil business began to recover, work as a landman and lease broker. My income sure as hell wasn't what it was as a vice president of a bank in San Francisco, but it was enough for me to live on in Cordell.

M.B.'s condition continued to worsen. He looked terrible and would sit for long hours just staring out of the window at nothing. He scarcely ate at all and continued to lose weight. I tried to get him out of the house and interest him in something but without much success. His condition was doubly troublesome since he had always been a fighter, and I'd never known him to quit on anything in his life. Football season came and went, and he never went to Norman to see a game. He only went quail hunting once, because I insisted, but didn't show any enthusiasm for the hunt or the dogs he had always loved.

Then winter came, and one day M.B. disappeared. He wasn't at home, and I couldn't find him. His car was gone, so I assumed he'd be back, but when the evening passed and he didn't return, I began to worry. The next morning I alerted the police and the sheriff. The temperature was in the twenties with the wind making it even colder. It was three days later that a rancher about thirty miles away found the car. M.B. had apparently driven up a dirt road and parked. He wasn't in the car, and it took a few more hours to find him. He was dead, sitting on the ground with his back against a tree, dressed only in a thin jacket and pants. The autopsy concluded he had died of a combination of exposure, dehydration, and hypothermia. Like an old Indian, M.B. had simply decided it was time to die and, like every other problem in his life, taken care of it himself.

We buried him in the town graveyard. A preacher read a few prayers, and Don Ed delivered a short eulogy describing M.B. as an honorable man, which he proved again in the way he died, just as he had in the way he lived. After the funeral Don Ed said, "You know, Snake, dying is easy. It's living that's hard." I don't know if that was the case for M.B. but at that minute I knew what Don Ed meant.

Don Ed's wife fixed fried chicken, usually one of my favorites, but I didn't feel like eating. It wasn't so much sadness, but more a feeling of vacantness—like things in the world that should be right had been readjusted, and now were wrong.

Don Ed sensed my mood and did most of the talking. "Look, Snake, I was happy to say a few words about M.B.—he was like a father to me, too—but normally I hate funerals and I just don't go. When I had that heart attack, I had to recognize my own mortality. Before that I assumed I'd live forever, I was bulletproof and invincible. So I thought about death for, say, maybe ten minutes. Then it came to me—why bother? What I need to plan for is life, not death."

"However, I do have a few thoughts, and I want your help. You know my wife is a strong Methodist. She goes to church every Sunday, and I'm afraid she'll want some kind of formal funeral for me when I die. I don't want some sanctimonious preacher who didn't even know me making up shit to try and make me sound good. The last funeral I had to go to the minister even mispronounced the dead guy's name. Boy was that a moving ceremony. No, just cremate me and say to yourself one thing, 'Old Don Ed had a fighter's heart.' That's enough. Now eat your fried chicken or you'll insult my wife and I'll have to take you outside and whip your ass!"

That, at least, brought a smile out of me, and the chicken did taste a little better.

When I got home, for one of the few times in my life I felt lonely, so I sat down and wrote another poem for Don Ed.

I'll Walk to My Funeral

I'll walk to my funeral
I'd rather not ride
In a pine box
I'll be so long inside

I don't want an old picture
to top an obit
that's written by someone
who flunked English Lit.

Don't hire a preacher
to tell some big lies
like they always do
when a real sinner dies

I think I'll go out
the same way I came in
dressed up to die for
in my natural skin

Don't play any sad songs
or shed a sad tear
just think of me once
when you hoist your next beer

Don't spend any money
on some fancy coffin
it's just something
to carry me off in

I don't need a plot
that's walled and gated
just start a good fire
and be sure I'm cremated

Think of a eulogy
that's not too boring
I don't want to hear
the whole crowd snoring

If you must have a marker
don't mention my age
I'm older than dirt
but I still won't behave

So, I'll walk to my funeral
I'd rather not ride
in a pine box
I'll be so long inside

I showed the poem to Don Ed the next time I saw him at the courthouse.

"Snake, for a west-coast, liberal hippie, you catch on pretty good. It must be your sound, Oklahoma upbringing."

I think that meant he liked the poem.

We'd lost the bank, I'd lost my wife, and now I'd lost my only family. I did have a good friend in Don Ed and a good enemy in Duane Lucas. Time passed and I grew accustomed to my life. Cordell wasn't San Francisco, but it was home. There was no way to like the place, and no way not to like the people, except for Duane Lucas and then General Sherman—both of whom it turned out would continue to have a hold on my future.

CHAPTER 12

The sheriff stopped me as I came into the office and growled at me, "Don't bother to get comfortable. We've got work to do."

"What's up, Boss?"

"Morford won't get off of his place, and the bank can't take over the property. Floyd's getting pressure from Lucas to do something about it, and now he's riding my ass to enforce the foreclosure judgment. He's asked the judge to issue a writ of assistance and he wants Morford thrown off his land."

"Well, we can do it if we have to, can't we?"

"It's not that simple. Besides the politics of throwing Morford off the farm he and his family owned and worked for years, it looks dangerous. I've heard that Sherman character is out there heavily armed and has brought in help."

"Are we looking at another Waco?"

"We are if we're not careful. Red knows Morford's cousin. He's talked to him. He says Morford's willing to meet. I want you and Red to go with me. We need to see what's going on out there and if we can talk Morford into leaving."

"If Sherman's still there, I doubt it. That guy gives me the creeps."

"We've got a meeting at Morford's farm. Get Red and let's roll."

We took the sheriff's Ford Explorer and he drove. During the drive out we agreed that the sheriff would do all of the talking, Red would watch Sherman and anyone else who was there in case trouble started, and I would try to see what sort of firepower had been put together at the farm. We arrived at the gate to the farm and were faced by a homemade wooden sign the size of a small billboard which announced: "Free state of the United States—No trespassing."

"If it's so damn free, why can't people go in and out?" I popped off as we pulled up to the gate.

"Nobody likes a wiseass, Snake. I told you I'd do the talking," the sheriff replied.

Red got on the phone and called Morford's number at the farmhouse. In a few minutes a dilapidated truck topped the rise of the dirt road that led from Morford's house, throwing up dust as it wound its way to the gate. Two men I'd never seen before got out. They were dressed in khaki uniforms and carried sidearms. A deer rifle was racked behind the driver's seat, and the truck had an American flag sticker on the front bumper. One of the men approached us, opened the gate, and waved us through.

"General Sherman says he'll meet you at the house."

As we bumped down the road to Morford's house, Red and the sheriff agreed that they'd never before seen either of the truck's occupants. "Armed strangers. Boys, this doesn't look good," the sheriff said.

It didn't start looking any better, either. As we approached Morford's house, we saw a Humvee, painted military green, and several tents pitched on Morford's lawn. Another man stood in front of the house dressed in blue jeans and a cutoff sweatshirt. He had a huge knife on his hip and was carrying a high-powered rifle with a scope.

"Mornin', Sheriff. Welcome to a free country. Park right there, and I'll tell the general you're here."

Red looked at the man and after minute said, "Hey, Leland, how come you don't get a uniform? Still in basic training to be an asshole first class?"

Leland gave Red a hard look and the sheriff said, "Shut up, Red. I told you I'd do the talking."

We stood in the yard and faced Morford's small, white-framed house. The house and the yard were well cared for, as were the out buildings. It was a shame he had to lose the place, but the price of wheat just wouldn't pay the mortgage and leave enough left to live on.

Morford was a prime example of the small family farmer who beat his brains out working but couldn't quite make it in a global economy he could not control. Those farmers who could avoid a mortgage might get by from year to year—making money in good years and eking by in the bad ones. Drought, flood, bugs, crop diseases, and the markets that dictated the price of wheat, gasoline, and fertilizer ruled their lives. Morford had done all right until his daddy died and he had to either sell the farm or borrow money to pay estate taxes. He was land poor. The land was worth a lot, but he had no cash for taxes. He had gambled on borrowing the taxes and mortgaging his farm. Bad choice.

Morford and General Sherman came out of the house. As they approached, I tried to figure out what it was that bothered me so much about Sherman. He was big, but that wasn't it. It was his eyes. They were as cold as I'd ever seen. I have never seen a wolverine, but I've heard they're the most vicious of all animals. His eyes would have done justice to a wolverine.

"Hello, Sheriff. Welcome to the free state."

"I came to talk to Morford," the sheriff replied.

"I'm in command here. You'll talk to me. State your business."

In spite of Sherman's statement, the sheriff made a point of directing his remarks to Morford. He may have looked soft, but I knew from experience he was tough when it counted and not to be taken lightly. If you pushed Sheriff Checker, he pushed back.

"Morford, you're going to have to get off this property. I don't like it, but that's the law, and I have to enforce the law. You'll have to make arrangements to move. You don't own the land anymore, the bank does."

Morford did not reply, but the general did.

"As freemen, we do not recognize the illegal acts of your bankrupt and unauthorized court. Mr. Morford lives in a free state. We are here to defend his rights."

"Mr. Sherman, the law applies to you as well. I don't want trouble, but Mr. Morford has to leave the property. Don't threaten me, or I'll have you in that unauthorized jail down there in Cordell, America. Do you understand?"

General Sherman drew himself up to attention, looked at the sheriff, and stated, "This meeting is over. Please leave the property or we will consider you a trespasser."

"We'll leave, but when we come back, and we will come back, Morford had best be gone," the sheriff replied.

During this exchange I had been trying to move around where I could case the joint. I saw enough tents for as many as eight or ten men. I was pretty sure I saw someone at the window of Morford's house, probably covering us with a weapon. Also there were three other vehicles pulled up near the barn.

"Come on, boys," the sheriff said as he motioned Red and me back to his car.

The truck followed us off the property. I could tell the sheriff was really mad by his silence and the way he drove.

"That son of a bitch can't take the law in his own hands, but we've got to be careful. I don't want anybody killed over a piece of real estate."

"Particularly when it belongs to Duane Lucas," I said.

"There's a pair to deal to. He and Sherman are two of a kind, as mean as they get. And by the way, I didn't meet Leland in Sunday school," Red chimed in. "He nearly beat a man to death with a chain over by Lone Wolf. He's a bad-ass biker and dumb enough to be dangerous."

"I tried to look around, Sheriff. I think there are at least eight or ten of those paramilitary types out there. If we go in with force, a lot of people may get hurt."

The sheriff drove for a few miles, and after visibly calming himself down said, "This is going to take some planning and some help. I'll consult the DA when we get back. We sure don't want violence if it can be avoided."

"Wouldn't you know Lucas would be the cause?" I replied.

"One of our problems is all we have to enforce is an order in a civil suit. Maybe these guys will screw up and commit a crime," Red said.

"Or maybe they already have," I added. "Let's run them through the computer to see if any of 'em have a record. There may be warrants out for their arrest, or they might be felons on parole, or probation, who can't have guns in their possession. Then we can get the DA to help and get a warrant for an arrest."

But when we ran Sherman and Leland through the computer, we found nothing helpful. Leland had a number of misdemeanors and traffic tickets, but no felonies and no outstanding warrants. Sherman had no record at all.

"So, we're back to square one," the sheriff said. "I'm going to consult the DA and the judge. We've got to be careful not to start a war out there if it can be avoided."

On my way home I had another idea for getting information on Sherman. Mike had told me he still had "connections" with the CIA from his Vietnam days. Although he was full of bullshit, he had been known to deliver on some unlikely promises, so I saw no harm in giving his source a try. When I called Mike, he was glad to help and told me he would contact his old friend who had stayed in the agency after Vietnam. As usual, I didn't know when I'd hear from Mike again, but figured it would be when I least expected.

CHAPTER 13

I was in Arapahoe, the county seat of Custer County, checking title on the ownership of some mineral interests for an oil company out of Amarillo. I had one of the big, heavy index books open on my lap where I was sitting in the hall outside the county clerk's office, immersed in my job, when the clerk called me to the phone. It turned out to be Don Ed's bailiff.

"The judge wants to see you, Snake. He's been looking for you all day."

"Tell him I'm busy over here in Arapahoe trying to make a living and stay off the welfare roll. I'll drop by when I finish this project."

"No, Snake, that won't do. He wants to see you today. He says it is important."

"Tell him I'll drop what I'm doing—but not on my toe, it's too heavy—and I'll be there this afternoon."

I got my notes together, replaced the index book, and started for Cordell some forty miles away. When I arrived at Don Ed's court, he was on the bench hearing some kind of case that involved three sets of lawyers. I went into the courtroom and sat down in the last row of spectator seats. It took the judge a few minutes to notice me, but when he did, he called a recess and motioned me back to his chambers as he left the bench.

When I entered his office, Don Ed was sitting behind his desk still dressed in his black robe. On the wall behind Don Ed was a poem I had written for him. Don Ed had the poem framed. It was called "The Lawyer."

THE LAWYER

A Lawyer died today.
They say he passed away,
without a sound.
I know that it's not true,
for it would never do,
for even God
to have the last word.
He left little estate, and
only one last wish,
to be buried standing up,
so that he'd arrive in Hell
ready to give
his opening statement
to the devil.

"Sit down, Snake. I need your help. I've been worrying about a case, and I need to do something about it."

"Well, you do look a little older, Don Ed, so maybe you have been worrying."

That caused Don Ed to get an expression on his face that I knew too well. What looked like a thin smile really meant, "Go to hell, smart-ass."

"Snake, I'll be old when I say I'm old and not a minute sooner. Right now I expect to die before that happens."

"Only the good die young, so at least you're old enough."

"Thanks for the encouragement, but I really do need your help."

Don Ed then went on to tell me the story of one of his last cases as a lawyer before he took the bench. A taxi cab driver had been killed in Oklahoma City. His body was found in a vacant lot near his abandoned cab. The driver had been stabbed twenty-two times, including fatal wounds to his throat and heart.

The accused was a black crack dealer named Case, who was well known on the east side of Oklahoma City as "Crankcase." His prints were identified in the cab, and he was in possession of the taxi driver's credit cards when he was arrested. The murder weapon was never found, but Crankcase was prosecuted for first-degree murder.

Crankcase admitted stealing the cards from the driver, but adamantly denied the murder, insisting he came upon the body while walking home to his apartment. The jury didn't believe him, and not only found him guilty, but gave him the death penalty.

Don Ed took over the case on appeal, claiming among other issues that the defendant had ineffective counsel at trial. The Court of Criminal Appeals agreed with Don Ed's arguments, reversed the decision, and ordered a new trial. Although the briefs had been filed before Don Ed went on the bench, the appellate court had not issued its decision until after Don Ed became a judge.

Crankcase had told both his original lawyer and Don Ed that he had an alibi witness who he was with at the time the murder was committed. The first lawyer apparently didn't believe Crankcase and made no effort to find the witness. The case was now scheduled for a retrial and Crankcase was being defended by the public defender. The public defender did not have the resources to look for the witness, who, according to Crankcase, was a young, white woman who told him her name was Angel. She had come to the east side of town to buy crack and then they had gone to Crankcase's apartment to smoke dope for several hours just at the time when the driver had been killed.

Although even Don Ed was originally skeptical of Crankcase's story, in the manner of all zealots, he had convinced himself that it might be true. And if the witness could be found, Crankcase could establish an alibi and prove his innocence.

"So, Snake, I want you to find the witness," Don Ed concluded.

"Whoa there, Judge. Isn't this the old needle in the haystack? We don't even know if this person really exists, or her name. And furthermore, this all happened five years ago. If she's a crack addict, she's probably dead."

"Or in jail, which would make her easy to find for a sleuth like you, Snake," Don Ed replied.

"Judge, you know I'd do anything for you, but is this scumbag worth saving? Assuming I could find the witness, she testified, and anyone believed her—all of which I doubt."

"No one deserves the death penalty. And even though I can't defend this man any longer because I'm a judge, I owe him the best defense available, and that includes an attempt to verify his alibi."

"Well I guess I could try. It's not as though I have a whole lot going on in my spare time. I'll have to interview Crankcase. Which jail is he in?"

"He's over at Granite, and I've already arranged with the warden for you to see him. Here's the number to call to set up an appointment. Good luck. I've got to get back to court and finish this trial. Let me know if you find out anything."

Don Ed was one of those rare people who can put pressure on you to succeed without saying a word. He had given me a job, and he expected me to accomplish the assigned task. Somehow he made me know it was my responsibility to find the missing witness. He had his job to do, and I had mine. If I failed, I would have to accept total responsibility. It was as though he had created an inexorable duty that could not be shirked without fear of failure. I can't explain how he was able to create this feeling, but he did. That meant I couldn't give up until I either found the witness or proved no such person existed.

And so I added one more title to my growing resume. Now I was a private investigator. I felt like I ought to buy a trench coat and try to look tough, but instead I just thought the project was a big waste of time. If anybody but Don Ed had asked for my help, I would have refused. But for Don Ed, I had to at least try.

CHAPTER 14

Shortly, I was on my way to Granite to see Crankcase. In the hour or so it took to make the drive, I alternated between kicking myself for taking on a time-consuming and probably futile job, and congratulating myself for being loyal to a friend. In the end, I decided to try the positive approach and apply my best effort to finding the witness who probably didn't exist.

The positive thoughts lasted until I reached the main gate of the prison. Granite is a maximum-security prison. That means I had to be let in through the gates by armed guards, pass through a metal detector, and even take off my shoes and be patted down before I could enter. The guard who acted as my host was about five feet, five inches tall and weighed every bit of three hundred pounds. He addressed me as Shay-riff and apologized profusely for having to take my gun and search me.

Once inside, I was seated in a small, windowless room with a metal table and two metal chairs. The door to the room was also metal and contained a thick glass window set at about head height. In a few minutes the guard brought in Crankcase. He was a little, wiry-looking black man with two tattoos, one on his right arm that said "Crank" and the other on his left that said "Poison." When he smiled, he showed a gold upper tooth right in the center of his mouth.

Crankcase extended his hand and, with a salesman's smile, announced, "Pleased to meet you. Any friend of Don Ed's is a friend of mine."

"I call him Judge, and I'm not your friend. I intend to try to help you because of the judge, who may be the only friend you have in the world. If you cooperate with me, I may be able to help. If not, I won't, and you'll get the death penalty, which you probably deserve. Now, sit down and answer my questions."

"No need to come on like a hard-ass. I know you're on my side, and I know it's because of the judge," Crankcase stated with special emphasis on the word judge. "I'm innocent, and I will cooperate."

"That's what I need to hear. Sit down and answer my questions. I want to know all about the night of the murder and your alibi witness."

"I didn't do no murder. I sold crack and smack, but I didn't kill nobody. I never carried no knife. You hear what I'm sayin'?"

"I hear. Now, tell me your tale."

"That mother fucker that they call a DA down there in his cowboy boots and western string tie strutted all over the courtroom, and my pissant, little white lawyer, and that white judge, let him run all over me. You hear what I'm sayin'? Mother fuckin' lawyer didn't even object and didn't know shit. If it weren't for Don Ed—I mean, the judge—I'd be a dead motherfucker already. You hear what I'm sayin'?"

"Crankcase, I hear you. Stick to the story."

So Crankcase told me his version of the night of the murder. As usual he had gone to a nightclub where they played jazz and blues. It was largely a black place, but some white people came in to hear the music or score drugs.

About nine o'clock, a skinny, white woman in her thirties with the haunted look of an addict came into the club. Crankcase had seen her before and sold her drugs on several occasions. She looked nervous and strung out, and as soon as she recognized Crankcase, she approached him and asked him to meet her outside. Outside, standing in an alley next door to the club, she told him she wanted to buy a rock. She knew the price was forty dollars, but she was broke. She said she had a good camera she'd trade for a rock, and it was worth way more than forty dollars. After looking over the camera, they made a deal. Crankcase sold her the crack and went back to the bar where he sipped scotch and waters and listened to the music.

Around midnight he walked out of the club to talk on his cell phone about another drug deal, and the woman showed up again. She pleaded with Crankcase for another rock and offered him a somewhat worn jacket for the dope. Crankcase refused and started back inside, and that's when the crackhead said she'd give him a blowjob for the rock. After some playing around, they got in her car and drove to his apartment, which was not too far from the club. Once there, she delivered on her end of the bargain and so did Crankcase. They sat around and listened to music, and she smoked the rock in a little glass pipe she carried in her pocket. About 5:00 a.m. she drove him to a 7-11 to get cigarettes, and while he was inside, drove away without explanation.

Crankcase then started for home, walking. On his way he saw the victim's cab, parked with the door on the driver's side open. Then he spotted the body of the driver in a vacant lot about thirty yards from the car. Crankcase said the driver was dead. He examined the body and found nothing of value. He searched through the cab, leaving his fingerprints, and found the driver's wallet, containing a credit card but no cash, on the floor in the backseat. He took the wallet and later used the credit card to buy a stereo.

A record of his prints was on file with the police, and when the taxi was examined, his prints were found and matched. The police arrested Crankcase and found the driver's credit card in his possession. The medical examiner fixed the time of death at around 2:00 a.m. The cab had been called to the nightclub where Crankcase had been seen, and his only defense was his own story and an alibi witness, who not only couldn't be found, but was also a drug addict, if she even existed.

After listening to his tale, I told Crankcase, "The judge is the best criminal defense lawyer in this part of the country, and maybe in the whole United States, but even he couldn't get you off with that phony alibi story. I think I'm wasting my time."

"It's true. The judge believes me. You can prove it if you find the bitch. I was with her until 5:00 a.m. I couldn't have killed that motherfucker. I've done some bad shit, but no murder. You hear what I'm sayin'?"

I sat back a minute and reminded myself why I was there, and after a little reflection addressed the poor, wrongly accused Mr. Case.

"Okay, let's assume your story is true. Where do I start to look for this girl? First of all, what was her name?"

"Shit, man, they don't never give their real name. She called herself Angel, said she was sent from heaven. You hear what I'm sayin'?"

"What did she look like? Could you recognize her?"

"Man, all you white folks look alike, but my life depends on this. I could recognize her white ass, if you could find her."

"I need a lead. Think about what you know about her. What kind of car did she drive? What did she look like? Anything you can think of to help find her."

"She drove some kind of old, piece-of-shit car. A Chevy around an '82 or '83. She said it was her roommate's."

"What else do you remember about her?"

"She had a belly button ring."

"What else?"

"A tattoo. The bitch had a little angel playing a harp tattooed on her ass—a little angel on one cheek."

I continued to question Crankcase about times or places he had seen Angel before, but he couldn't add anything helpful.

When I left the prison, I thought about how to begin my search. I could go to every bar in Oklahoma City, look for skinny, white women, and ask them to drop their panties and show me their butt. It might be fun, but didn't sound like a very good investigatory plan. I'd have to think of something else.

CHAPTER 15

After being in the prison, I needed to get outside. Those four, cold walls shutting me in away from the sky and the sun depressed me, even though I could leave. So, instead of going directly back to Cordell, I headed for Quartz Mountain State Park, just about fifteen miles southeast of Granite.

Quartz Mountain is a unique place for Oklahoma. A series of steep rock piles rise above the otherwise uniformly flat landscape. Not really tall enough to be mountains, these hills are reminiscent of the Arizona desert, and are uniquely isolated in one small cluster stuck into the southwest part of the state. A man-made reservoir had been created in the center of the mountains, and a state lodge on the shore of the lake hosts the prestigious Oklahoma Arts Institute, where gifted and talented teenagers meet each summer to study music, dance, poetry, and other artistic disciplines. The roller coaster road leading into the lodge from the highway for about six miles is a good place for a run.

So after changing clothes at the lodge, I set out on a hilly, six-mile run up the road leading into the park. It was a weekday, and there was virtually no traffic on the road as I toiled up the first steep hill toward a rocky notch where the road crests. Six or eight turkey buzzards soared on huge wings above the crest of the hill, floating and diving on the up and down drafts that circulate above the rock formations strewn along the road.

I huffed and puffed my way out of the park itself and onto the road that leads toward Granite. As I passed into a clump of black jack trees, two deer ran across the road about fifty yards away. I turned at a 65 mph sign that, through experience, I had learned marked a spot about three miles from the lodge, and as I ran back through the stand of trees, heard a wild turkey gobble somewhere off the road.

When you are running, you develop a rhythm and a pace, sometimes a little slower, sometimes a little faster. You soon learn that the body is not a machine that can simply be turned on and run the same everyday. Injuries, fatigue, or simply state of mind can effect how you run. When feeling strong on a clear, cool day, it seems that you can run forever, but one of Oklahoma's hot summer scorchers may force you to use all of your will power to simply gut out a few slow miles. In any case, I always seemed to feel better for making the effort.

This was a good day because of the scenery and the relief from the stark reality of the prison. But due to the heat, by the time I got back to the lodge I was pouring sweat and tired, even though I was feeling like the world was a far better place than it had been when I left Granite. I sat down on the front porch of the lodge, drinking water and just enjoying the warm sun, clear sky, and fresh air of western Oklahoma. This was a place where there was still enough space for humans, birds, and wild animals to coexist. Too bad it had to be spoiled with a prison, but Crankcase and his pals had to live somewhere.

Before I left, I stopped by to talk to the park ranger, a good-looking, blond woman, who lived in Altus. I always made up an excuse to ask her a question about the park, but the real question was whether she was still living with her boyfriend, and the answer—that she was—caused me to keep right on moving north toward Cordell. I stopped at the only gas station in Lone Wolf, picked up a beer and a bag of pretzels to console me on the way home, and hit the road at the recognized western Oklahoma speed limit of eighty-five miles per hour.

CHAPTER 16

Red and I were just returning from repossessing a car out in Kiowa County. Next to domestic disputes, repoing cars was probably more likely to turn dangerous than almost any other task associated with my job. A few years before, one of the deputies had been shot at by a disgruntled car owner whose car was being repoed and had to kill the shooter to save his life. Fortunately, this time the repo had gone smoothly.

We were walking toward the courthouse when a stranger approached. He wore an ill-fitting sport coat and wrinkled slacks that looked about three sizes too big. He was short and sported a scruffy looking beard, which along with his hair was beginning to turn from brown to gray. He smiled and handed me his card, which identified him as a reporter for the *Dallas Morning News.*

"I'd like to talk to you boys for a minute."

"Talk away," Red responded.

"I understand that there is a problem out at Morford's farm. What do you intend to do about it?"

"I don't know what you mean by problem," I responded.

"I was out there and talked to a fellow named Sherman. He called himself General and said Morford and his farm were not part of this state, nor, in his words, subject to "our corrupt and bankrupt judicial system." The courthouse shows there is a judgment requiring Morford to turn the farm over to the bank. Do you intend to enforce that judgment?"

Before I could respond, Red shot an arc of tobacco toward the reporter, which with practiced accuracy, narrowly missed his foot and said, "Hell, yes!"

I interrupted and said, "We work for Sheriff Checker. You'll have to talk to him."

"It looks to me like if you go out there to enforce that judgment, there's going to be trouble. Are you ready for that?"

"Look, I told you to talk to the sheriff."

"He said no comment."

"Then that's what we say. How'd you hear about this in the first place?"

"Everything that happens in Cordell is big news in Dallas. I just came up to cover the bake sale over at the church and one of the ladies mentioned Morford and Sherman."

"You're about as funny as a case of the flu," Red said.

"Well, if you boys ever want to talk, I'll keep it off the record. I might even buy you a beer."

"We'll buy our own beer," I responded as we headed into the courthouse. "What do you think about that?" I said to Red as we walked up the stairs to the sheriff's office.

"I don't like it. Getting the press involved puts the sheriff on the hot seat."

When we entered the office, the sheriff was on the phone. He looked agitated, and as he hung up, he said, "Some reporter from the Dallas paper was just here asking about Morford. I think Lucas called him, or maybe that damn general tipped him off. In any event, I don't want anyone talking to him until we have a plan."

"You're the boss, but we can't let those assholes defy the law forever," Red responded.

"I agree with that, and I've set up a meeting with the highway patrol in Oklahoma City to see if we can get some help. Snake, I want you to go with me. You know that guy the governor appointed as commissioner of public safety. He was a friend of M.B.'s. We're going to see him day after tomorrow."

CHAPTER 17

Two days later the sheriff and I took off to see the commissioner of public safety in Oklahoma City. The commissioner of public safety is the head of the highway patrol and is appointed by the governor. The appointment is political and the person who gets it doesn't always know how to handle the job. In this case, Glenn Smith did. He'd grown up with the governor in Tulsa, but had spent his whole career in law enforcement, first as an MP during the Vietnam War, and then on the highway patrol. One of his patrol assignments had been in Washita County, and that's how he came to be acquainted with M.B.

Glenn's office was in a one-story brick building near the Oklahoma City Zoo. It was unpretentious, but so was Glenn. He ushered us in cordially and listened intently while the sheriff described the problem.

"Chubby, this is a real problem. I think we got us a Mexican standoff, and this sure doesn't make it any easier," Glenn stated as he tossed the sheriff a copy of the *Dallas Morning News*.

The paper had an article on the front of the second section with a headline, "Standoff in Washita County." The story mentioned both Ruby Ridge and Waco several times and tried to compare the situation.

"I'd like to help, but this deal is getting political. I have to talk to the attorney general, and maybe the governor. You know that damn Lucas was one of the governor's biggest financial supporters at the last election."

"That bastard turns up everywhere," I said.

"You got that right, Snake, and I'm sure he wants that farm. Chubby, what do you think happens if you go out there in force and try to put Morford off his land?"

"From the looks of things, we'll have one hell of a fight on our hands. Sherman and those other weirdos are armed, and I think they mean business. Morford may be in violation of the law, but he's a decent citizen. Putting him off his land is a little bit like the dust bowl days. You know, 'big banker takes farm from honest farmer by force.' I don't like it, and I don't want to see anyone get hurt over a piece of property."

"Well, there sure is no easy answer. Give me some time, and I'll get back to you. I hear you're getting pretty handy with that sidearm, Snake. Maybe you could just go in there like Clint Eastwood and take care of the whole thing," Glenn smiled.

"Thanks, Glenn. You're the one who's a cowboy at heart. I think you should straighten things out for the good of the great state of Oklahoma."

On the way out Glenn asked me about Don Ed.

"You know, when I was a highway patrolman I had to testify in a murder case. Don Ed represented the defendant and he cross-examined me. My ass was about four pounds lighter when I finally got off the stand, but for some damn reason I still liked that tough little son of a bitch. Give him my regards. We ought to have more lawyers like Don Ed. I bet he's a good judge."

"Don Ed would be a good anything. I'll give him your regards."

The sheriff and I left with another promise from Glenn that he would see if he could help.

I told the sheriff I was going to stay in Oklahoma City and work on finding Don Ed's lost witness and the sheriff caught a ride back to Cordell with Red, who had come in to pick up some new radar equipment to help catch speeders, as the tickets we gave were important to the county's revenue and supported the Court Fund.

Before I left highway patrol headquarters, I asked Glenn's assistant to run the names of my latest leads on Angel through the law enforcement computer system. I figured there would be a good chance of a drug conviction somewhere on her record, but at least under the names I'd found, I had no luck.

I decided I'd go talk to Leon, who owned and operated Leon's Barbeque located in an old gas station. Leon's had served great barbeque for as long as I could remember. Situated near the state capital on the east side of town in a black neighborhood, Leon had for years filled the stomachs of fat cats, legislators, and just ordinary people with the best barbequed ribs in the state and his signature banana cream cake.

Leon loved sports, and his restaurant was decorated with signed pictures of Oklahoma greats, from Mickey Mantle to Billy Sims. He even had a picture of a young quarterback with his hand raised in victory at the Rose Bowl, which I'd signed at his request. When I had time, I sometimes played golf with Leon at Lincoln Park, the public course not far from his restaurant, and when in town I nearly always made time for a plate of ribs and some of his famous cake. Leon knew everybody on the east side of Oklahoma City and what they were up to, good and bad. I figured he might know something that would give me a lead on the elusive Angel.

I arrived at Leon's just after the lunchtime rush and found him sitting at one of the dented and chipped linoleum-topped tables that, along with the great smells of steaming ribs, set off the ambiance of Leon's. He had on a short-sleeve golf shirt covered by a grease–spattered, white apron and was drinking a coke from a big, plastic, ice tea glass. The waitress brought me a plate of ribs, which I slathered with Leon's famous hot barbeque sauce and dug into while Leon listened to my story about the hunt for Angel. When I finished, Leon just looked at me and laughed.

"Snake, you got no idea how many young, white girls you see in this neighborhood at night. Hell, half of them are strung-out junkies, and the other half are rich kids hoping to score some cocaine or marijuana. None of 'em would use their own name, and unless they get busted or killed, there is no way to trace any of 'em.

You're wasting your time. Besides, Crankcase is a crack dealer and a worthless piece of shit. Why do you care about him?"

"I don't, but Don Ed does, and that's all I care about. Don Ed would try to save a cockroach from the death penalty."

"He'd have a better chance. I don't understand why he cares, but I do understand he's your friend and you're trying to help. I'll ask around. How are the ribs?"

"You're losing your touch. The sauce just isn't hot anymore. I'm almost through, and I've only had to drink three cokes and three glasses of water."

"I shouldn't have asked a white man, anyway. What the hell would you know about ribs?"

There was no reason trying to poke around on the east side of town. It would be a cold day in hell before a white law enforcement officer got anyone in that part of town to talk about a murder case, or anything to do with drugs or drug deals. As much as I hated it, I knew I'd have to talk to Crankcase again and see if he knew a black person who could go with me and try to get people to talk, although it would still be unlikely.

CHAPTER 18

I was out for an evening run, and I'd just turned around and started the homeward leg of my five miles. It was unseasonably hot and humid, and I was already tired and running slower than my normal pace. I didn't pay much attention to the vehicle that passed me going the other way, slowing down slightly as it went around me toward the yellow line.

That is, until I thought I heard the brakes. A minute later the Ford Explorer came idling up alongside.

The window on the passenger's side went down to reveal General Sherman. I got that same nervous feeling in the pit of my stomach that came on every time I encountered the general.

"Good to see you staying fit, Deputy."

"Sherman, we got nothing to talk about 'til you get off of Morford's farm."

"It is the duty of all citizens to defend the rights of freemen. I act only in the name of the Republic."

"Yeah, and I'm Abraham Lincoln."

"Don't smart-ass me, Deputy. I am serious in my beliefs. Change your attitude and join us in the fight to save our fundamental rights."

"Sherman, when do you think "no" really means "no?" How many ways can I say it to make you understand?"

"Suit yourself, Deputy," Sherman said as he accelerated and then disappeared down the road.

As I chugged along to finish my run, I contemplated whether he actually thought he could recruit me or if his appearance constituted a subtle threat, letting me know that he knew my habits and when I was vulnerable. It was an unsettling thought.

CHAPTER 19

I had some papers to serve over by Canute. I was in a hurry and still driving my Sheriff's vehicle, wearing my uniform and carrying my gun. The law in Oklahoma had been changed years ago so that legal process could be served by private individuals licensed by the state, and I didn't need to be in law enforcement to serve a legal document, on this occasion however, it turned out to be a good break.

I glanced at the document, which was a contempt citation for failure to pay child support. The State Department of Human Services had been supporting two children of a man named Steve Reynolds and wanted to drag Mr. Reynolds into court to make him reimburse the state for the monies paid out as support.

The defendant lived in a rundown trailer behind a convenience store at the end of the small town of Canute. I pulled the Explorer, with the sheriff's star on the side, up in front of the trailer and walked over and knocked on the flimsy door. After three attempts at knocking, the door flew open, and I was confronted by a big, burly-looking dude in a tank top, shorts, and no shoes. He had greasy hair, bloodshot eyes, and a dirty-looking handlebar mustache. The place reeked of pot and beer, and clearly Mr. Reynolds was stoned out of his gourd. More importantly, he had a tire iron poised at about shoulder level in his right hand. He stepped toward me and then—comprehending the uniform, badge, and gun—paused, but at the ready. Instinctively, my hand went to my gun, but I didn't back up an inch.

"Hold on there, padnah. You don't want to get shot over some child support papers," I said as I flexed my legs and got ready to draw and dodge if I needed to move quickly.

"Fuck you. What do you want?" mustache mumbled.

"Are you Steve Reynolds?"

"Who the fuck wants to know?"

"The DHS. And here is an order for you to appear in court."

He still held the tire iron, but he didn't look quite as ready to use it, more disoriented, but still dangerous.

I tossed the paper down between us on the floor of the trailer.

"You can stick your damn paper up your ass, pussy," Reynolds said as he kicked at the papers with one bare foot, which caused him to stumble sideways, giving me a chance to step back down the front step of the trailer as he slammed the door in my face.

As I drove back to Cordell, I thought about the last time I'd been in a fight. If you didn't count subduing a few drunks or prisoners, it was my freshman year in college, but I remembered it well. When I got to Stanford and started football practice, I quickly acquired the nickname of "Okie," being much too shy to bring up my high school nickname of Snake. For the most part, "Okie" was the source of good-natured kidding, and no offense was intended nor taken, with one exception.

The biggest and best player on the team was a hulking defensive tackle from Lodi. Kurt Keorkorian was an Armenian. He weighed about three hundred pounds, shaved his head, lifted huge weights, and was downright nasty. Kurt decided to make my life miserable. When he called me Okie, he said it in a way that always carried an insult. He let me know he considered me a member of a lower class of subhumans. Furthermore, he wouldn't let up—he rode me constantly.

One day after a long, hot practice, we were in the locker room and Keorkorian looked at me and said, "Okie, get me a drink of water. You know about dry from the dust bowl."

"Get your own damn drink," I replied.

"Don't talk back to me, Okie. I grew up with a bunch of one-suspender, trailer park, white trash like you. They all fucked sheep or goats and married their cousins," was his reply.

I shut down. I couldn't see, I couldn't hear. All I could do was hit him. I landed a good punch right below his jaw, in his neck. It shook him, but he didn't go down. He bull-rushed me and smashed me into a locker, bear-hugging me with a hold that was intended to break my ribs. I tried to hit him, but he was too close and my blows had no effect. Just as I was about to lose consciousness from lack of air, three other players pulled him off of me long enough that I could stagger free.

He stepped back and looked at me with a death-head grin.

"I'll get you, you Okie piece of shit!"

I had no air in my lungs to reply.

I let the incident slide, and after the coaches talked to Keorkorian, he pretty much ignored me, until a few days later when we were scrimmaging before our opener against San Jose State. I was taking snaps as the third-team quarterback and spent most of practice on the sidelines playing catch, or trying to get a glimpse of the girls' soccer team practicing on an adjacent field, but near the end of practice the coach called my name to enter the scrimmage.

To avoid injury in practice, the quarterbacks wore red vests over their practice shirts as a signal that they were not to have any contact. Keorkorian was lined up as defensive tackle. As I faded back to throw, he gave me that same death-head grin. I thought I could feel pressure from behind and stepped up as I threw over the middle, but too late.

Keorkorian blindsided me and drove me into the ground, coming down on me with all of his weight. It was my first concussion. I couldn't get up. I had to be carried off the field, and I was out of football for two weeks. The coaches disciplined Keorkorian, but couldn't do too much, as they needed him too badly. Maybe I was lucky. He left me alone after that, and I soon found he was pretty much hated by everyone on the team, even before hitting me with his cheap shot. The next year he went to the NFL, and three years later he was shot and killed in a bar in Atlanta after attacking a bartender with a broken beer bottle.

CHAPTER 20

I didn't have any good ideas for helping the sheriff with Morford or finding Angel, so I decided to drive out to Black Mesa and hike to the top. It was the highest point in Oklahoma, which wasn't very high—only a little over 4,900 feet above sea level—but I had never been there and had heard it was really beautiful and different from anything else in the state.

Black Mesa is stuck in the extreme northwest corner of the Oklahoma panhandle only a few miles from Kansas, Colorado, and Texas and, at the top, only a few hundred yards from New Mexico. Even from Cordell it was a drive of over four hours. The first part was largely boring, tearing along through the flat Oklahoma prairie. Then, just west of Boise City, the tiny county seat of Cimarron County, the whole environment changed into a desert-like ecosystem, with scraggly mesquite trees, cactus, and rocky, sandy soil, like nothing else in the state.

When I reached Black Mesa and began my hike to the top, the drive seemed well worthwhile. The mesa itself had a purple cast, setoff by exposed rock and dirt, and the desertlike terrain was sprinkled with wiry, green bushes and some sparse grasses. The climb to the top was only two miles and mildly strenuous. What surprised me was the vast size of the top of the mesa. It was almost two miles more across the top to reach a monument marking the highest point in the state from where you could see into four other states. New Mexico was so close that I walked into it just for the hell of it.

There were quail everywhere. Not the usual bobwhites, but scaled quail, which are blue with a topknot. They stuck close to the ground and sometimes ran rather than flew when startled by my passing. The quail reminded me of M.B., and for a few moments I missed him intensely. Besides OU football, M.B.'s passion was quail hunting. He kept good dogs and had a trainer he considered the best in Oklahoma. When I was about twelve he bought me a cheap, twenty-gauge shotgun and let me go with him. During quail season he hunted at least three or four days a week, and on weekends I always tagged along.

M.B. was only a fair shot. He shot an old Browning Sweet Sixteen with beautiful etching on the breech, even though sixteen-gauge shells were uncommon. It was a beautiful gun, and I still have it, because it reminds me of him.

M.B. went hunting more to enjoy being outside than he did for the actual shooting. He loved walking and watching the dogs work. He seemed to like the slow pace of the hunt through the open fields more than the intense action of the frantic covey rise and the thunder of the hunter's gun in response. There was something about the open country and the freedom of the outdoors that took him away from his day-to-day responsibilities of running the bank and separated him from his otherwise rigid and structured life. Even though deer and wild turkey hunting were popular in western Oklahoma, M.B. disdained these activities. He found sitting in a blind for hours boring, and said there was no sport in hitting a large animal with a scoped rifle, or a huge bird at close range with a twelve-gauge shotgun. It was the dogs, the movement, and the ritual of quail hunting that attracted him back year after year.

His dogs were always in good shape, and they would range far ahead, leaping through the grass and brush until they finally smelled birds. Then they began a relentless pursuit of the scent with noses to the ground, ending in a rigid point, signaling the trailing hunters to hurry forward with guns at the ready to honor the dogs' efforts.

To me the fun of the hunt began at covey rise when the quail exploded in all directions, flying at startling angles. It took quick reactions and a good eye to hit the fast and erratic target the birds presented. Over time my anticipation improved and my young reflexes allowed me to almost always hit at least one bird, and frequently double out of the same covey.

The dogs would retrieve the downed birds and then begin to hunt for the single birds which had spread out over the wide fields and were often located hundreds of yards away. This is where the real merits of M.B.'s fine dogs showed. The dogs would pick up the scent of a single or perhaps two or three birds and track them to another point, giving the hunters a chance to bring down the remaining birds one at a time. This shooting also took skill and some judgment. As the hunters spread out, it was easy to make a quick move only to find M.B. or his trainer in my sights and decline to fire at the elusive flying bird.

Hunting and football were both part of the fabric of life in western Oklahoma, and fall was an exciting time, particularly as I grew taller and stronger and began to play junior high and then high school football. I never played anything on offense but quarterback. It just seemed to come naturally that I could throw. I had a live arm and always wanted to get my hands on the ball and control the game. Our school was small enough that most players played both ways, and I was no exception. On defense I played strong safety. Because of the level of competition, I was more than adequate, but my real love was quarterback and throwing the ball.

Along with the rodeo, football and hunting constitute the test of manhood in the small towns scattered across the vast, open spaces of western Oklahoma. I never took to the rodeo, being essentially a town boy and not living on a farm, but football and quail hunting became an important part of my life and proved that I could be trusted to become a man on terms my peers understood.

Those thoughts lead me to compose a poem. I called it "The Hunt."

THE HUNT

Dogs and guns and endless plains.
Thin winter sunshine,
laced with whirring
birds in covey rise.
Something grows and
something dies.
Time suspended
for a day.
Things proceed
in a bygone way.
Nothing different in
the hunt.
Boyhood, manhood,
age all blend
cherished sameness
to the end.

Like most of my poetry, it was written to please myself, and I'm not sure I ever even showed it to anyone else.

CHAPTER 21

I met Mike while trying to save the bank. I had to get to Santa Fe fast to meet a rich developer who said he was interested in buying the bank. He wasn't a great prospect, but I had to try. Someone told me about Mike's charter service, and I hired him to fly me out to New Mexico. Mike entertained me all the way there and back with stories of his service in "Viet Nam" and accounts of his flying adventures. Even though the trip was unsuccessful, I got a kick out of Mike and his constant line of chatter. He invited me to play basketball at Weatherford in a pickup game that happened every Thursday night. It was some months before I had the time to take up Mike's invitation, but both Mike and the game quickly became fixtures in my life.

When I learned that Mike was a crop duster as well as a charter pilot, I started nagging him to take me for a ride. Mike advised me it was illegal to take a passenger in his crop dusting airplane, and that his insurance wouldn't cover a passenger in the plane, but I finally wore him down and he agreed to take me up.

Mike might be crazy on the ground, but as he said, when it comes to flying, "I'm dead sober, and dead serious, so I won't wind up dead. I hate to fly with anyone else, Snake, because I'm the very best pilot in the world. I just don't trust anyone like I trust myself. You may think I'm crazy on the ground, but in the air you couldn't find a better pilot."

The day we were to fly turned out perfect—sunny and not too windy. Mike picked me up in his battered pickup. He always had some bizarre bumper sticker on his truck. The current one read, "There is no gravity the Earth Sucks."

"What the hell does that mean?" I asked.

"I haven't got the vaguest idea, but I think it's cool," Mike replied.

We drove over to Weatherford where Mike kept his plane. On the way to Weatherford Mike talked about crop dusting, or what was now referred to as the Ag business, or Ag flying, by those involved. The first crop dusting was done in old bi-wing planes after World War I. Later, converted Piper and Stearman aircraft were used. The first plane designed for crop dusting was the Snow S1 built by hand by a Texan named Leland Snow who was twenty-one years old at the time. Leland built the plane himself with wood and canvas wings. There was a demand for that kind of aircraft, and he soon began to build metal-wing planes known as S2s. These planes became extremely popular, even though the first prototype almost killed its designer when the wing blew off in an air stress test and Snow was forced to bail out of a spinning, disintegrating aircraft at low altitude. Somehow he survived, although future models were stress tested on the ground, not in the air. Snow's company, now known as Ag Tractor, still makes state-of-the-art Ag business aircraft, in various sizes, at their plant in Olney, Texas. Leland is the dean of the business and a great flyer and designer. Unfortunately, Mike said, these aircraft are now too expensive for a small operator like him.

Mike himself flew an old Cessna Agwagon, circa the 1970s, that would make about 120 knots and had a stall speed around 65 or 70 knots, although that was deceptive since it stalled at different speeds depending on the load the plan was carrying. The Cessna was equipped with a tank for dispensing chemicals that would hold two hundred gallons. When full, it added weight to the aircraft, which further complicated the flying. I asked Mike which was the most dangerous part of his job and what caused accidents. Without hesitation he immediately responded "wires."

"You've got to look for poles, not wires. You're going too fast and you're too close to see the wires. Where there are poles, there are wires, and that's what you have to locate before you start your application. For the most part, you can cut the wires with your prop or with the wire cutters that are on the wings, tail, and the cockpit of the airplane, but that's sure not true if you hit a "smokey," one of the big cross-country electric wires that are more cable than wire. A smokey will flat bring you down."

According to Mike, the business is not near as dangerous as people think. There are only about twenty-five serious accidents every year in the United States, and only twelve to fourteen of these results in fatalities. Mike's view was that this wasn't very many considering the number of pilots, around five thousand, and the number of hours they fly.

He admitted to only one crash. A few years back he went to West Texas to fly in a government subsidized boll weevil project. He was flying somebody else's aircraft, in territory with which he was unfamiliar. He scouted the field where he was going to apply the pesticides and counted two power lines. Unfortunately, he didn't see a third line which ran along a major highway but was setback some distance from the farmer's field where he would apply his load. Coming in on his descent he counted two lines and then began his dive to set the plane down near the ground, to release his load. His wing hit a pole holding the third line, shearing the wing off and causing him to crash into the field, sliding for several hundred yards. Miraculously he survived with only cuts and bruises and walked away from the cockpit, which was all that was left of the plane.

His crash in West Texas caused Mike to vow to become a "stay at home" pilot. He only flew in areas where he was familiar with his customers and the known hazards. According to Mike this made his flying much safer. As I was to learn shortly, safer is all relative.

Mike's plane was equipped with a GPS devise which allowed him to keep careful track of how he laid down the chemicals and provided an accurate guide for his work. Prior to the GPS, Ag flyers had used people as spotters on the ground, smoke, and even paper stringers to keep track of the path of the application of their load. All of these were subject to some inaccuracies, particularly in the wind and led to many claims by neighbors for damages due to chemicals dropped, or being blown, onto their land. The GPS was a truly positive innovation in the business.

As we turned into the strip where Mike kept his plane, he couldn't resist telling me the real danger of his business was having to find a new wife or a girlfriend every season.

"When I'm working at crop dusting for four to five months in a row, I work seven days a week, twelve to fourteen hours a day. I can make really good money, some years as much as a hundred fifty thousand, but the problem is I lose a girlfriend or wife every season."

"Well, from what I hear, Mike, there are some of them that would just as soon see you hit some of those wires you fly over."

"You're probably right, Snake, but let's go flying."

Crop dusters are careful people. This may come as a surprise, since they rank near the top in the hierarchy of dangerous jobs, but like many true professionals who routinely risk their lives, crop dusters are careful about their equipment and their safety. They know that what they do every day is inherently life threatening, and though they are willing to trust their own ability when it comes to flying, they don't want to die because of a poorly maintained aircraft. Their lives depend on the reliable performance of the planes they fly, and Mike, like most crop dusters, maintained his old Cessna meticulously, even though it had over seven thousand hours of flight time.

When I looked at the cockpit I couldn't believe two people could fit. It was about the size of a theater seat. "Have you ever taken anyone else up in this?"

"A few women," Mike smiled.

"I don't want to sit on you're lap."

"If you want to ride, then squeeze in side by side."

I crammed into the plane next to Mike and we took off. We flew around for a few minutes, performing steep turns, dives, and climbs until Mike sighted the field he was looking for to show me how the plane performed.

"Look for poles, not wires, Snake," Mike reminded as he suddenly started a steep dive. Just before it seemed we would plow straight ahead into the ground, he leveled out parallel to the field and brought us in under some electric wires that could not have been more than twenty feet above the ground. The landing gears were almost touching the ground, in what he described as a "high pass." It seemed we had just flattened out horizontal when we shot straight up just in time to pass over another set of wires at the other end of the field, then making a "race-track" turn 180° to the right followed by a sudden 270° turn to the left. I didn't throw up, but I must have turned a few shades of white as Mike got a good laugh out of my appearance.

"You don't look like you want to be a crop duster, Snake. Maybe you'll learn to like being a deputy sheriff."

"I think I've got the picture, Mike. And you're right, being a deputy sheriff doesn't look so bad. If you would have taken those Vietcong flying with you, you would of scared them all to death, and we probably would have won the war."

Mike made a few more passes at the field and then cruised on back for a perfect landing at his home strip. I crawled off the plane a little unsteadily, glad to be back on the ground.

"Just tell me when you want to go up again, Snake. Next time I'll load up the chemicals and you'll see what it's really like to fly one of these babies fully loaded."

"Flying is dangerous enough, Mike, but don't you worry about those toxic chemicals you're around all the time?"

"Hell, Snake, I've put so many chemical substances in my body over the years, it's just a race to see which one kills me first. One more dangerous substance won't change my odds on dying, which are already 100 percent."

"Yeah, but what about other people who might be exposed to those pesticides?"

"The way I lay them down, there's almost no chance they get out of the field. Besides, I'm tired of you fucking tree huggers who would rather go without food than see farmers make a crop to help feed the world. Hell, that shirt you have on would have probably been boll weevil bait if some guy like me hadn't laid down pesticide on a cotton field."

"Anyway, Snake, you sure as hell know by now that life is just a trade off between decisions. There's consequences to every decision, you just have to live with them. I know you're a half-assed idealist, but I've never seen you wimp out when it came down to decision time. You just worry to damn much. You need a new girlfriend."

"Thanks a lot, Mike, for all your wisdom. I thought I came out here for a plane ride, not a lecture. Let's go get a beer."

The flight sure hadn't made me want to be a crop duster, but it did make me realize that Mike was a great pilot. Reassuring, at least, if I was going flying with him again.

CHAPTER 22

The next Saturday I was eating breakfast with Red and one of the other deputies at the café. On Saturday mornings I usually got up early and ran ten miles and then went to the café for pancakes. Red would often meet me there, having just dug himself out of bed after sleeping off his Friday night drinking and partying. He had a sort-of girlfriend he called the Widow Woman who lived over near Bessie. They would go out to some country-and-western joint and drink beer and line dance almost every Friday night. I could tell how much Red had to drink the night before by the number of cups of coffee he drank and the amount of syrup he put on his pancakes. This Friday must have been a hell of a night, because he was flooding his plate with syrup and gulping down his fourth cup of coffee.

"I'll tell you what, Snake, that damn Widow Woman danced my ass off last night. Then she got me drunk and made me take her home and fuck her socks off. I'm getting too old for this kind of life."

"I think you're braggin', not complainin', Red."

"Maybe so, but let me tell you, this deal with Morford is getting worse all the time. Everybody at Cowboy's wanted to know what we were going to do about movin' him off his place. Half the people say we'd be Nazi pigs if we do anything about it, and the other half say we're pussies for not enforcing the law. I don't envy the sheriff on this one. They've got him in a Wewoka switch."

"Rumor has it you want to be the sheriff when the boss retires."

"That's whiskey talking, Snake. You know that dog won't hunt. I ain't no politician. I wouldn't know how to handle this Morford deal at all."

"I see it coming to a head soon. The media is focused on it now, and they won't let up until something happens. That Dallas reporter puts an article in the paper every chance he gets, the *Daily Oklahoman* is following the story too and so is TV. I still think Sherman may do something that gives us probable cause to go in and arrest him on criminal charges."

We went to the cash register to pay our bill, but before we could get our money out we saw what looked like a flyer or handbill on the counter. It consisted of large black letters that said:

"WACO
RUBY RIDGE
DON'T LET CORDELL BECOME ANOTHER
VICTIM OF THE FEDERAL GOVERNMENT.
THE UNITED STATES HAS FALLIN' INTO
ENEMY HANDS IN WASHINGTON, D.C.
SAVE THE REPUBLIC. SUPPORT
JOE MORFORD, A TRUE PATRIOT."

"Where did you get this?" I inquired of the girl at the cash register.

"They're all over town," she replied. "No one is taking credit for them, but from what I hear, a lot of people agree that Morford is getting a raw deal. Some of the older folks say it makes them remember the dust bowl when the banks foreclosed everybody out of their property. What's the sheriff planning to do about Morford and that Sherman guy?"

"I don't know, myself, but he'll handle it so no one gets hurt. I'm sure of that."

We paid our bill and started to leave when Red punched my arm and pointed across the street.

"Shit, Snake, there's another one."

As we exited the café, a TV truck equipped with a satellite dish and bearing the logo of an Oklahoma City television channel was pulling into a parking spot by the courthouse. It looked like things were going to get worse before they got better for Sheriff Checker.

CHAPTER 23

Mike and I were headed for Guthrie to take in an evening at the Blue Grass Festival. Guthrie is one of the oldest towns in Oklahoma. I like the feel of the place, with brick streets and buildings, mostly built after the Oklahoma Land Run of 1889. The residents have worked to restore the downtown area and have done a good job of preserving the historic look with almost no encroachment of modern-looking structures.

There are a number of Victorian-looking bed and breakfasts and restaurants. Most of these are a little too cute for my taste, but I certainly do like the Blue Bell Bar, where Tom Mix was the bartender before he headed for Hollywood and fame on the silver screen. The town is also blessed by one of the best fiddle players of all time, Byron Berline, who also makes fiddles at a shop located in front of a music hall where he appears a few nights a month. Byron has played with everybody from Bill Monroe to Eric Clapton and is responsible for promoting the Blue Grass Festival.

The Festival was held on the high school athletic field. It was a cool, clear night and Willie Nelson was the featured attraction. In fact, that was the only reason Mike was willing to go to the concert. He normally didn't like blue grass or country music, but he had great admiration for Willie. As Mike put it, "Willie is the only person I know who truly does not give a shit. Besides, he advocates smoking grass every day for your health. How could anyone possibly not like a man who is that philosophically sound?"

I liked Willie as well, but I did have one complaint about his show. His agenda was always the same. He played old favorites that the crowd loved and wanted to hear, but his repertoire never changed. It was as if he was suspended in time, or perhaps had been pickled and came out only to play and then retreat back within yesterday's world.

We sat on a blanket and drank beer listening to the preliminary acts, and then to Willie and his band. It was a fine, relaxing night, and I was enjoying the evening. That is, until Willie stopped for an announcement between songs. He said he had always been interested in the plight of family farmers, and as everyone knew, he did an annual concert for Farm Aid. He had heard about an honest man in Oklahoma who was about to lose his farm to a greedy banker, and he wanted to dedicate a song to Joe Morford of Cordell, Oklahoma. He then sang the old Woody Guthrie song "Pretty Boy Floyd," which favorably compared outlaws to bankers.

At the end of the song a group near the stage jumped up waving American and Confederate flags and cheering wildly. I saw the flash of a camera and recognized the Dallas newspaper reporter, who was photographing both Willie and the demonstrators. I tried not to let it ruin my evening, but it did show how serious and widespread the sheriff's problem was becoming. Spurred on by the media, the standoff at Morford's farm was becoming a national incident.

On the way home, Mike drove and I wrote a song about Willie. Obviously, I still liked him in spite of his politics. It went like this:

THE SINGER

A singer of songs,
a teller of tales,
sending a message,
without the need of the mails.

Voice full of gravel,
or just Texas dust,
words flowing slowly,
like watching iron rust.

Don't Never Shoot Short

Music that's made in the soul
and the heart,
words that are special,
and tell the hard part.

Songs that he's written,
and songs that he's sung,
remind us of dying
and life just begun.

Not just those ballads
of phrases so trite,
but rather sad sounds,
to rehear in the night.

Tuned by the thoughts
of a much-traveled brain,
playing and singing,
that brings such sweet pain.

Years, and not days,
that have happened before.
All of the feelings
that walked out the door.

Leaving behind
Only thoughts, that remain
Too silent and personal
to make the refrain,

Of songs that tell stories
of love won, and love lost,
of bandits defeated,
regardless of costs.

But the wind blowing now
through the still moving dust
leaves the message quite clear,
he is one of us.

A man, that's for sure,
more human that most,
with a talent for playing
and singing, almost.

A singer of songs,
a teller of tales,
sending a message,
without need of the mails.

"You know, Snake, you're about a half-assed writer, but that's better than no ass at all." Like Willie, I really didn't give a shit what Mike thought.

CHAPTER 24

Mike called, as always, at an inconvenient time, and insisted that it was important that I meet him at the Bonanza Bar near Hobart. I'd never heard of the place and asked him why we couldn't get together at T-Bone's or someplace else nearer to home. He said he had heard from Sally, and she had told Freight Train about Mike, so he was trying to lay low for a while. Even though I was busy, when he said he had some information on General Sherman, I agreed to meet.

The Bonanza Bar was a dump. A gravel parking lot fronted a low, sheet metal building painted a faded green with a corrugated tin roof. The portable sign in front of the place said, "Cold lon necks $1.00 at appy Hour." There were quite a few cars in the parking lot, but that was always deceptive, since half a person usually comes in each car parked in front of any bar.

Inside, the place was no better. A couple of well-worn pool tables, a juke box, and a few scattered tables. The interior was dark, dingy, and smelled of old cigarette smoke and stale beer. The few patrons looked like they were there because they had absolutely no place else to go and nothing else to do.

Mike wasn't there yet, so I sat at the bar and ordered a beer from the bartender, who was dressed in old work shirt and worn blue jeans. There were several people sitting in the back, but it was dark enough that I couldn't really identify any of them. Three men sat at a table behind me and near the bar. They all wore cowboy hats, boots, and jeans. One looked vaguely familiar, although at first I couldn't place him. He was burly looking with a black handlebar mustache.

All of the men looked like they had been drinking, and the table where they sat was covered with empty beer bottles. I kept trying to place Mustache, but it didn't hit me who he was until I began to hear his conversation with the others.

"That's the pussy that served me with child support papers. I hear he's a big lawman over at Cordell. He don't look so damn big to me."

Then I remembered Mustache was the guy I'd served papers on at a trailer park on the outskirts of Canute. I looked over at the table, which was my first mistake. Mustache sat in his chair with his legs stretched out and crossed like he owned the place. One of his companions had a flattened out nose that clearly had been broken a few times, and when he opened his mouth, was missing two teeth on one side. The other man at the table was big and wide with a thick neck and bulging shoulders. The toothless one gave me a nasty smile.

"He's a deputy sheriff over in Washita County, but that don't mean shit over here in Kiowa County," Mustache continued.

"Hey, pussy, what you doin' here? Trying to serve somebody else with divorce papers, or did you just get tired of playing with yourself?"

Turning back to the bar, I tried to ignore what was being said, but I knew what was coming, especially when Toothless said, "I heard them deputies over there at Cordell was candy asses. They're scared of old Morford and his friends. They talk big, but they don't want to get their asses whipped by a bunch of farmers. Ain't that right, pussy?"

When I did not reply, Mustache chimed in, "Hey, my friend's talking to you, asshole. Are your disrespecting my friend?"

I didn't need a bar fight, especially not with three drunk, hostile rednecks, so I decided to ignore them, pay my bill, and get out alive, but they were having none of that. When I turned to leave, Mustache was unfolding out of his chair, and Toothless was also getting up, but neither one of them got far. A huge bulk of a man moved forward from somewhere near the back of the bar and stepped in between me and Mustache. It took me only a second to recognize Freight Train.

"You boys aren't lookin' for trouble with my friend here, are you?" the big man said in a calm voice.

"Hey, this ain't your fight, big man. Step aside."

"If I say it is, then it is," Freight Train replied.

Instead of backing down, Mustache sprang sideways and aimed a vicious kick at Freight Train's knee. Freight Train, moving with the nimble quickness of a dancing bear, sidestepped the kick and landed a punch to Mustache's face that sounded like a baseball bat hitting a watermelon. Blood flew everywhere, and Mustache pitched backward across the table and onto the floor. As Toothless came across the table with a knife in his hand, Freight Train snatched a metal chair and brought it down across his knife arm with such force you could hear the bone break. He then whipped the chair back across Toothless' face, knocking him to his knees, where he let out a strangled sound and pitched forward on his face.

The third man at the table never moved and simply looked up at Freight Train and said, "You knocked the shit out of those ol' boys."

"Jesus, Freight Train, thanks. They were getting ready to beat the shit out of me."

"You ought to stay out of a dump like this, Snake. What the hell are you doing here?"

"Let's get out of here and talk outside," I responded.

"Fine with me, I just stopped in to take a piss in the first place. You're lucky your dad and I were friends, or I would have just watched the action. Those boys meant to hurt you, Snake. They're no damn good."

"You got that right."

When we got to the parking lot, Freight Train got in an oilfield pickup, and I went to my car. I thought I saw Mike's old truck slow down and then speed up again as it passed the parking lot. Maybe he was even luckier than I was. In any event, at this point, it was every man for himself.

CHAPTER 25

I was only back in the office a few minutes before I got a call from Mike.

"Boy, am I lucky. What the hell was Freight Train doing in that dump?"

"I'm not sure, but you damn near got me killed. If he hadn't been there, I would have been in big trouble." I proceeded to tell Mike about the fight and Freight Train's part in saving me from a bad beating.

I concluded by asking, "For God's sake, why did you want to meet in that joint?"

"I have some information on General Sherman. I'll come over and tell you what I've found."

Mike arrived and, after what I thought was a less than adequate apology, assumed his best conspiratorial tone and told me what he had found out about Sherman. Mike's old Vietnam buddy who had stayed in the CIA had access to information that was otherwise classified. Sherman had a file with the agency, and it was revealing. His real name was Emanuel Wortz and he was no general. He was born in Los Angeles in 1955 and served one hitch in the Army as an enlisted man seeing action in Somalia. He applied for the Army Rangers but was turned down for psychological reasons and didn't re-up. After leaving the Army, he adopted the name Sherman and served as a mercenary in Mozambique and Columbia. He turned up later in Miami as the bodyguard for an international arms dealer.

The CIA file also revealed he had connections with at least two paramilitary type militia organizations and a white supremacy group in Idaho. Although Wortz/Sherman had no criminal record, he was suspected in connection with an armed robbery in Texas, but there was not enough evidence to file charges.

The file also documented unexplained trips by Sherman to Afghanistan, Pakistan, and Cyprus. Most recently he had run an ad in the *Wall Street Journal* identifying himself as an expert in personal and corporate security with a Las Vegas post office box to receive inquiries. In short, the CIA concluded that Sherman was dangerous and associated with potentially violent groups.

None of this news served to help matters with the situation at Morford's farm, and although Mike's paranoia was probably more because of Freight Train than any of this information on Sherman, I did understand why he wanted to be careful. I kept my promise to Mike and didn't reveal the source, but did pass the information on to the sheriff. We agreed that about all it accomplished was to confirm that Sherman and the others at Morford's were armed and potentially dangerous.

Mike didn't call for a while. He didn't even show up at basketball, which showed how much he was afraid of Freight Train. Having seen the big man in action, I didn't blame Mike for staying out of sight.

In the meantime, the Morford case began to draw more and more attention from the media. The liberal press was confused. On the one hand, Morford was the victim, crushed down by the bank for reasons beyond his control, but on the other hand, he was supported by a bunch of gun-toting right-wingers who exemplified everything the lefties loved to hate. In spite of any confusion as to whom the good guys really were, the story made news. And since it could be sensationalized, it was picked up by the national media.

The mood around the office was bad as winter turned into spring. Early spring in Oklahoma is ugly, with cold winds blowing down across the unprotected plains. As Red liked to say, "There's nothing between here and the North Pole but a barbwire fence." The season was also marked by violent electric storms and, sometimes, tornadoes. Later in the spring it would get warmer, with the trees and grass turning green, and be one of the best times of the year. But through March and into April, the wind would howl across dry plains, pushing red Oklahoma dust into the air in what could be choking clouds.

All of us deputies wanted to get the Morford case over with as much as we wanted the weather to change. The sheriff didn't act, but you could tell he was getting restless too, and I felt like something would happen soon.

CHAPTER 26

Back in San Francisco for a friend's wedding, I was reminded of how much I loved the place. There was always something romantic and mysterious about San Francisco. I expected to see Jack Kerouac or Charlie Chan step out of the fog or maybe get offered the Maltese Falcon by a sinister man in a black suit. My only problem was that the memories there were almost too much for me sometimes.

My thoughts of Kit were still bittersweet. I imagined her walking into the room with her aggressive, springy stride and giving me that smile I could not resist, that was somehow both sarcastic and seductive. Of course, it never happened. I'd seen *Casablanca* too many times. But just the thought of running into Kit added a certain level of excitement to being in San Francisco, which had an edge all its own.

This time I was waiting for a friend in the Washington Square Bar and Grill, one of my favorite places in San Francisco. The "Wash Bag" featured an old style bar within a habitual crowd of hard-drinking sports fans. The much-used wooden bar is manned by professional bartenders full of jokes and stories about San Francisco athletes and characters, and some nights jazz is playing. The place is populated by a wide cross section of politicians, professionals, and just neighborhood hangers-on, which creates a lively scene.

I was downing a cold anchor steam, and instead of thinking of Kit, I thought about Julie, the only real girlfriend I'd had since my divorce. She lived in Oklahoma City and turned out to be as crazy as the Mad Hatter. We had been together off and on for three years until we finally broke up for good. We would fight and separate, and then go back together, and fight and separate, over and over. I thought I was in love with her, even though I knew somehow it would never work out in the end. My friends never understood that I loved her because she was crazy, and not in spite of it. I still missed her, so I dreamed up yet another song and wrote it down on a napkin.

I JUST SAW YOU FOR THE FIRST TIME, SINCE I SAW YOU FOR THE LAST TIME, WHEN I SWORE I'D NEVER SEE YOU AGAIN

I just saw you for the first time
Since I saw you for the last time
When I swore I'd never see you again.

You've been seen with who you're seein' and
I know you may be leavin'
So I guess I better see if you'll be seein' me again.

'Cause I remember sounds of laughter
And the quiet that came after
I swore I'd never see you again.

Comin' back may be deceivin'
And it may just lead to leavin'
And more times I won't be seein' you again.

But the comin' and the goin'
Lets me know what I've been knowin'
That this may not be the last time
I won't be seeing you again.

I just saw you for the first time
Since I saw you for the last time
When I swore I'd never see you again.

My friend from Stanford showed up and liked the song, especially when I told him it didn't apply to him and his fiancée. He said it sounded like a county-and-western song and probably belonged to Oklahoma, not San Francisco.

CHAPTER 27

The report of the crime was all over the newspapers and television. Four men dressed in fatigues and wearing ski masks had stolen a truckload of armament from a National Guard armory in Arkansas. The loot included rocket launchers, grenades, automatic weapons, and ammunition. Two National Guardsmen at the armory had been shot and killed. Before one of the guardsmen died, he was able to recount that at least two of the robbers were speaking in a foreign language, probably Arabic.

There was a nationwide manhunt on for the perpetrators of the crime, but few clues existed. The truck, its contents, and the criminals had disappeared, leaving almost no leads. It was clearly a professionally planned job, carried out by a ruthless and well-trained group acting with military precision and willing to kill to obtain their objective.

Although it sounded like the criminals had ties to the Middle East, the way they operated made me uneasy. Every time I thought about what happened, I started visualizing Sherman or someone trained by Sherman committing the crime. It seemed like a perfect caper for the general, and he certainly had Middle Eastern ties in his background. I even brought it up to the sheriff. He was a little more dubious about any involvement by Sherman, but didn't rule out the possibility. The sheriff did call Glen and ask him to stay current on the investigation and advise us if any evidence turned up that would link Sherman to the crime. If Sherman did take part in the robbery, it meant the freemen were even more heavily armed and our job was even more dangerous.

It seemed like matters just kept getting more serious when it came to the standoff, without any immediate solution in sight.

CHAPTER 28

The trip to San Francisco had relaxed me, but I was still literally without a clue on how to find Angel, and the Morford situation looked unchanged. Mike and I were in T-Bone's after basketball. Mike was talking about his last ex-wife. It seems she had sought counseling from a psychiatrist to help her deal with their marital problems. Her money probably would have been better spent on a contract with a hit man.

"You know, Snake, that shrinkhead told her my problem was that I 'objectified' women. When she told me, I asked her if that meant I wasn't going to get laid anymore. That was sort of the beginning of the end, or maybe even the end itself. She moved out right after that and took my favorite chair with her just out of spite."

"Yeah, and you miss the chair more than you do her."

"No. I actually miss her every now and then. She cooked the best Mexican food I ever ate, and sometimes I miss her enchiladas and chilies, not to mention her nice set of tits."

"There you go objectifying again, you male chauvinist pig. Why are women attracted to you at all?"

"It sure isn't my good looks. I think they like the fact I risk my life almost every day flying that crop duster. There's something about the danger that turns them on, in spite of my craziness and bad habits."

"One of these days you're going to plow right into the ground, the way you fly."

"We're all going to die of something. I'm over fifty years old. The Vietcong couldn't kill me, and I haven't killed myself yet, flying that crop duster. I can't be worried about dying, although I got to admit, Freight Train was hazardous to my life. Besides, do you want to die in a hospital with diapers on and a tube up your nose? I didn't know your Dad, but I respect him. He was an honorable man who knew how to die. I hope you're as good a man as he was."

"I'm damn sure not, but you're sure right about my Dad."

"By the way, Sherman and those freemen are a lot more dangerous than Freight Train. He might beat the crap out of me, but they'll kill you for a lot less than screwin' their wife."

"Thanks for the encouragement. You'll be surprised to know we may have a plan for those guys."

"Sure, and Janet Reno had a plan for Waco. I know Chubby is a whole lot smarter than Madame Fuck Up, but I can't see how he's going to handle this deal."

"With plenty of patience—something you wouldn't understand. But those guys do bother me sometimes."

"You worry too much, son. Drink your beer and don't cry in it. By the way, I've got a new girlfriend. She lives down in Oklahoma City. She's a little too skinny, but she's rich, or at least she will be rich."

"Yeah, and you're handsome. How do you know she's rich? You've told me a thousand times that women lie to you."

"'Cause I know her daddy, and he's rich."

"Okay, I'll bite. Who's her daddy?"

"Your pal, Duane Lucas."

"I can't believe it. I never heard he had children. I'd rather be poor than admit Lucas was my father."

"The reason you didn't know Lucas had a daughter is because she was so wild he wouldn't have anything to do with her. Now she's straightened out, he's talking to her again."

"If she's anything like her daddy, I wouldn't trust her."

"I think this may be my next wife, Snake. Maybe even my last wife. I've always wanted a jet. This is my chance."

"What makes you think Lucas would give anybody money, even his kin?"

"Taxes. Lucas hates taxes. Apparently he set up a trust for her many years ago to avoid taxes. There are millions in the trust, and she gets part of it at forty. She'll be forty in about three months."

"For you to stay with any woman for three months is a bad bet."

"I've thought about that, but I'm going to make it by using visualization."

"What do you mean by that?"

"Every time I start to do something foolish, I'm going to visualize that Learjet taking off with me at the controls. That's visualization."

"Are you going to introduce me to her?"

"Only if you keep your hands to yourself. I'm going down to the city this Friday. If you want to go with me, you can meet her. She won't come out here 'cause she doesn't like seeing her dad."

"Maybe I'll like her. We seem to have something in common. I guess I'll go with you. I need to check a lead on Don Ed's missing witness."

"Are you still chasing that ghost? Give it up!"

"Not yet. I'd like to find a new woman myself."

"You'll have to do it for yourself. Nothing in life ever comes to you, Snake. You've got to go out and get it. You want to eat something, you got to hunt it down first. Pun intended."

"You're right about that, Mike, even though you may wish you hadn't caught what you were hunting."

"This conversation is way too deep for me, Snake. Let's talk basketball or politics. It gets scary when I start agreeing with you on anything. Why don't you try to convince me that Oklahoma State has a chance to win the NCAA? Those Cowboys always choke."

We then degenerated into an endless argument that neither one of us could ever win.

CHAPTER 29

The next morning, after a breakfast of bad coffee and a banana, I walked into the sheriff's office at about 9:00 a.m. to pick up a subpoena the DA needed served in a criminal case.

The sheriff threw a copy of *USA TODAY* at me and said disgustedly, "Look at this. The SOB has God on his side now."

"What are you talking about?"

"'The Reverend Ezekiel Brown from Tennessee is now living at Morford's farm. He's carrying a 357 magnum and says he'll bring down God's wrath on anyone who tries to interfere with Morford's right to peaceful possession of his property. He came all the way from Memphis just to help this poor, honest man who is the victim of the Godless forces of our illegal and unholy justice system.' Can you believe this horseshit?"

"It was that *60 Minutes* show that did it, Sheriff. The press is a bunch of weasels."

"This just makes it that much harder to enforce the law. If we go out there in force now, we'll look like a bunch of Nazis," the sheriff replied.

"You still can't get any help from the feds?"

"No way. I even talked to our congressman. He says that since Ruby Ridge and Waco, the Justice Department is scared shitless they'll get more bad publicity. The chief FBI agent in Oklahoma City is sympathetic, but can't make a move without authority from Washington.

"If we have patience, Sheriff, they may screw up and commit a crime. That Sherman's belligerent as hell."

"Maybe you're right, Snake, but in the meantime Lucas wants me to force Morford off of his land."

"Tell him, no way," I replied.

"No, you tell him. You and I have a meeting with him at his bank in Elk City at 10:30."

"I can't wait. I need to see Lucas every now and then to remind myself how rotten he really is."

"Yes, but he's still got a lot of political clout. Money talks."

"Yeah, and bullshit walks. You know Lucas' secret to success, don't you, Sheriff?"

"Lay it on me, oh Great Carnac."

"He is 100 percent totally focused on money. He gets up thinking about money. He goes to bed thinking about money. Hell, he probably gets off thinking about money. It's all he cares about. You'd be rich too if all you did was think about ways to make money and didn't waste time on food, or football, or country-and-western music, or Don Ed's court reporter."

"Now, now, boy, you're risking a demerit for insubordination, but I think your theory is probably right. Let's go see the great man."

I glanced at the Holiday Inn as we drove into Elk City, another monument to Lucas' insatiable greed and cunning. Some years ago a real estate developer from Dallas with the inappropriate nickname "Lucky" approached Lucas with the idea of building a nice motel in Elk City. He wanted Lucas' bank to make a loan on the project. Lucky had even located the site, optioned the land, and had a preliminary set of plans drawn.

Lucas' reception was enthusiastic. He told Lucky he would even be interested in investing his own money in the motel, but needed time to study all of the documents and conduct some market research. Lucky left all of his information with Lucas and returned home elated about his chances for developing the project. He continued to be optimistic over the next few weeks as Lucas requested more and more information and finally talked about drawing up a contract for a joint venture, which included Lucas as a partner.

Then suddenly, Lucas would not return Lucky's telephone calls. Frustrated, he went to Elk City to talk to Lucas personally, only to be advised that, after further review, Lucas had decided the motel was not economically feasible. Realizing his option on the property was running out, Lucky went to the property owners and tried to extend the option. Strangely they refused, even though he offered a higher price. Without time left on the option, it was too late to find other financing. The whole deal disintegrated and Lucky—although furious with Lucas—having no legal recourse, abandoned the project and went back to Dallas to pursue other ventures.

That was the end of the story until over a year later, the fated Lucky was driving west on I-40 headed for a family vacation in Colorado. As he approached Elk City, he began to recall the story of his failed venture and was prepared to point out the proposed location to his wife. What loomed before him, however, was not the vacant field he fully expected, but a brand spanking new Holiday Inn. After he got over the idea that what he was seeing was not a mirage or a dream, Lucky decided to investigate and turned off the highway to the hotel.

As he approached the desk clerk she told him that she was sorry, but they were full for the night.

"Who owns this place?" Lucky asked.

"Why, Duane Lucas, of course. Mr. Lucas owns just about everything west of El Reno."

Of course, the bilked and frustrated developer brought suit against Lucas. What he didn't understand was that lawsuits are part of the sleazy banker's stock and trade. Lucas hired a huge, expensive law firm and began to literally law his opponent to death, swamping Lucky's lawyers with depositions, motions, and endless delays. Finally, after three frustrating years with the case still not to trial and Lucky nearly broke from the cost of his legal bills, Lucas settled for a token amount, probably not more than a few months' profits from his hotel.

Seeing the hotel and recalling its history at least put me on guard for the meeting with his great eminence.

We arrived right on time for our appointment with Duane Lucas. Lucas' bank was located in a nice-looking shopping center property he had picked up in foreclosure, when the owner ran out of money before finishing construction.

We were greeted by Lucas' secretary, an officious, older woman who had a reputation for stonewalling callers and guests Lucas wanted to avoid. She brought us coffee in expensive-looking China cups that carried the initials DL, seated us in a reception room, and advised Lucas we had arrived.

In a few minutes we were shown into Lucas' office. His office had a hardwood floor, oriental carpets, and paneled walls. Pictures of Lucas with governors, senators, and even President Reagan were everywhere. Trophies of the heads of deer, elk, moose, and javelina were on the walls.

Lucas' desk was raised above the level of the floor so that, in spite of his short stature, he looked down at the visitor from a high vantage point. The desk was a huge, antique railroad desk constructed before dictation machines, so that a secretary could sit on one side to take dictation on a stenographic pad across a wide, polished expanse from the person sitting opposite. Lucas sat empirically behind the desk in a high-backed chair. He was dressed in an expensive suit and a bow tie. When we entered, he rose and shook hands with the sheriff and then offered me his hand. I shook Lucas' hand and immediately felt guilty and hypocritical. The sheriff and I took our seats in the visitors' chairs set in front and slightly beneath Lucas' regal appearing desk and chair.

In his usual, unctuous tone, Lucas addressed the sheriff.

"Sheriff Checker, I believe in getting right down to business. I'd like to know when you are going to evict Morford so that I can take possession of my property."

"Mr. Lucas, this is a tricky situation. We have to proceed with caution so that no one gets hurt," the sheriff replied.

"Of course I'm sympathetic to that, Sheriff, and I am a patient man, but I have waited long enough. The court says it's my property, and I want to take possession. Those men out there are outlaws. I expect you and your deputies to enforce the law." As he referred to deputies, Lucas looked pointedly in my direction, and I stared back at him with my best dead-eyed look.

"It's not that simple, Mr. Lucas. There's a lot involved here. We don't want violence over a simple foreclosure case."

"Sheriff, I understand this is political, and I understand politics. I've talked to the governor, and he says the highway patrol will help if there's a crime involved. My lawyers tell me that trespassing is a crime. Also, I can't believe some of those men out there don't have a record. Have you checked on their criminal records?"

I could see the sheriff trying to control his temper as he composed himself and replied, "Mr. Lucas, I know how to do my job. Yes, I have checked, and none of the men at Morford's farm are felons, nor are there warrants out for their arrest."

"Sheriff, that's impossible. I'm told this Sherman character is a known terrorist. He must be wanted for something, and if he's not, I expect you to see that he is shortly. I want my land. I don't mind reminding you that you run for office next fall, and that you might just draw a well-financed opponent if you don't take care of this matter. That's politics, Sheriff."

"No, that's bullshit," the sheriff said as he got up from his chair and leaned across Lucas' huge desk, making me remember why I liked working for him. "Mr. Lucas, I came over here as a courtesy to you. I'll run my office without your help any damn way I see fit. Don't you ever threaten me again, politically or any other way."

Turning, the sheriff said, "Come on, Snake, this meeting is over."

Lucas, to his credit, never lost his composure and never moved from behind his desk, but only gazed out at us as though we were inferior creatures who he knew could be dealt with as he saw fit.

When we got to the car, I looked at the sheriff and said, "I'm proud of you, Boss, but what in the hell do we do now?"

"That's what I've got to figure out, Snake. Right now, I don't have a clue."

"We'll think of something, Sheriff. Let's talk to Glen again and see what he thinks."

Back at the sheriff's office, we called Glen, and the sheriff told him about our meeting with Lucas. Glen said the governor had called him and wanted him to help, but they had agreed the patrol would only get involved if a crime had been committed. After some discussion about bringing charges for criminal trespass, the sheriff hung up without reaching a conclusion and told me to go back to my duties.

After the meeting with Lucas, the Morford case took on a new meaning. Now it was a personal problem that had to be solved. At least my reaction was positive. I felt like Lucas would be vindicated in his criticism of the sheriff's department if we failed to evict Morford. I realized Lucas would get what he wanted if Morford was forced to turn over the land, but somehow the important thing was that we carried out our job successfully. In his twisted way, maybe Lucas has succeeded in motivating both the sheriff and me to carry out his wishes.

I could tell that the sheriff felt the same way, but his concern over hurting anyone on either side still made him reluctant to act, and the stalemate continued. With the weather improving as spring progressed, everyone began to feel better, even though the Morford case still affected the mood.

CHAPTER 30

Alonzo stopped me after basketball. He usually said very little and always disappeared right after the game, so I was surprised when he approached me and said, "Snake, can I talk to you? It's about my sister, Dawn. I'm worried about her. Maybe you can help."

"Sure, Alonzo, what's the problem?"

"Well, she has this little store over in Burns Flat. She sells gas, beer, pop, and some other stuff. Her husband ran off and left her ten years ago, and the store supports her and her kid. It's all she's got. She's goin' to lose the store."

"What do you mean, lose the store?"

"The woman who owned the store and rented it to my sister died, her daughter sold it, and the new landlord is going to raise the rent to more than my sister makes off of everything she sells."

"Does she have a lease?"

"She thought she did, but the new owner says it's no good and she can either pay more rent or get out."

"Well, Alonzo, I have a friend who's a lawyer who'll look at the lease and see what her rights are, and maybe I can talk to the new landlord. Who is it?"

"A rich guy named Lucas. He won't even talk to my sister. He just says pay or he'll kick her out."

"That son of a bitch is everywhere, like stink on shit. Get me the lease and I'll find out what your sister's rights really are, not what that lying bastard says. But I've got to tell you, he won't mind throwing her out in the cold."

"That's what we heard, but my sister doesn't know what to do. She can't pay more rent."

"I'll be up that way in the next few days. Tell Dawn I'll drop by and talk to her and pick up a copy of the lease."

"If anyone can help, I know it's you."

As Alonzo walked away, I could feel the anger and determination rising up inside. If there was any way to stop Lucas, I damn sure would give it a try.

It wasn't hard to find Dawn's store in Burns Flat. It was a small, cinder block building with four gas pumps in front, neon Miller and Budweiser signs in the windows, and a hand-lettered sign announcing "Hunting and Fishing Licenses sold here." The place was clean and well maintained, and inside was the normal array of pop, beer, milk, candy bars, snack foods, and cigarettes. Behind the cash register was a Native American woman. She was tall and slender with jet-black hair and the erect posture of a dancer or an athlete. She was so beautiful; I couldn't take my eyes off of her. Probably in her early thirties, she greeted me with a smile and identified herself as Dawn. As we talked we were interrupted several times by customers who bought gas and a group of teenage girls who took a long time shopping to end up with bags of chips and diet coke. All the customers were friendly and called Dawn by name, and she responded with a quip or a personal remark. It looked like the business was doing fine.

As we talked I became more and more mesmerized by Dawn, captivated by her dark brown eyes and her easy manner, although at times I detected an edge of sadness. She was clearly worried about her store, but was not whining or complaining, just concerned about her future and how she would support herself and her son. She seemed like a complex person, strong in some ways, but perhaps insecure in others. This aroused my curiosity and made her even more attractive.

Dawn did have a soiled and much-folded lease. It was on a printed form with the blanks filled in by handwriting. The lease was hard to read, but it looked to me like she had another three months on the lease term.

"What did Lucas say about having to get out of the store?"

"I never talked to Mr. Lucas. A vice president of his bank called, and then I got a letter demanding that I pay more or get out of the store. I've run this store for over ten years. It supports me and my son, but just barely. I have no savings, and I won't take welfare. There are no jobs in town. If I lose the store, I guess I'll have to move, but my only family is here and my son is happy and I don't want to leave. Can you talk to Mr. Lucas?"

"That's one thing I know won't help, but I'll have a lawyer look at the lease. He owes me a favor. Don't worry, we'll think of something."

Dawn seemed relieved when I left, even though the only thing I could see that might help her was a little more time on the lease. I knew I'd do something to try to help her, if for only to have an excuse to see her again.

Burns Flat wasn't exactly booming. There was almost nothing in the town but the school. On the way out of town, I did notice a vacant building that might have been an abandoned service station.

The assistant DA in Cordell wasn't too busy, except during jury terms, which usually only happened twice a year. He was allowed to have a private civil practice, as long as it didn't interfere with his duties as a district attorney. I asked him to take a look at the lease, and when he heard the story and learned Lucas was involved, he was not only willing, but eager to help.

CHAPTER 31

I was playing golf with Leon at Lincoln Park municipal golf course, near his barbeque joint. Leon loved to play golf at Lincoln Park, even though he could afford to play at a country club. It was the course where he learned to play. He had grown up caddying at Twin Hills Country Club, right across the street, and he could have bought a membership there, but he preferred Lincoln. The much-revered pro at Lincoln, U.C. Ferguson, had given Leon an old five iron when he was twelve years old, and Leon had found plenty of balls by searching the creeks and gullies of the heavily played municipal course. Leon would sneak onto the course just before dark and play a few holes with his one club. As a kid, his real love had been baseball, but he learned just enough about playing golf to be dangerous. He had a flat, powerful swing with a loop at the top, could drive the ball a long way in almost any direction, and was a lousy putter. I could usually lift a hundred dollars or so off of Leon, who consistently overestimated his ability.

Lincoln Park didn't favor his game, as it was a fairly tight course with trees and creeks lining and intersecting most of the holes. It was Leon's home course, and the home course to a regular group of golf hustlers.

One hole on the course is notable for an event that seemed to characterize Lincoln Park and the games that Leon played in there. Several years ago, two young black men walked out of the woods and approached a foursome on the fourth green. One pulled a gun and ordered the golfers to turn over their money and other valuables. One of the golfers, a local hustler at cards and golf, went to his golf bag to get what he said was his wallet, but instead pulled out his own gun. The young robbers fled before the hustler let fly, but the incident enhanced the reputation of the course as a rough and tumble gambling venue.

Leon had just taken a reckless chance by trying to drive a short, par four hole, and instead hooked his drive deep into a dense stand of blackjack trees. He was riding me hard for playing safe with a three iron tee shot when I asked him if he had any information on the elusive Angel.

"Snake, I don't know anything about that girl, if she even exists, but Don Ed may be right about Crankcase. That taxi driver had been messin' where he shouldn't been messin'. He was mixed up in some bad business with some bad people. The word is that one of the gangs had him taken out. Nobody ever heard of Crankcase carryin' or usin' a knife, but on the other hand, nobody cares about the worthless piece of shit; not even his momma."

"How do you expect him to prove he didn't do it without that alibi witness?" I responded.

"Ain't my problem. All I know is what I hear. Nobody cares if Crankcase gets the blame, and nobody remembers one particular, skinny-ass, white girl. Now, help me find my ball before you go try to play that chickenshit little bunt you laid out there in the fairway."

We finished the round and were sitting in the Cock of the Walk bar drinking beer. Leon was expounding on how the game of golf had changed since he first learned to play back in the fifties.

"Can you imagine what Ben Hogan would think about people riding around in little cars, hitting shots with huge metal clubs, dressed in short pants and pastel golf shirts? Personally, I don't have any quarrel with the new equipment. It makes the game way more enjoyable for most duffers, and who cares if the pros hit it 300 yards instead of 280 yards. But I guess because of being an old caddie, I can't get used to golf carts. Golf was meant to be played walking."

"Leon, golf is like everything else; it's based on money and designed for comfort. Besides, I like your titanium driver, because you hit it even wilder than your old driver. Come on, let's shoot some pool for that money you owe me from golf."

I brought up the subject of Crankcase to Leon again, but it was a waste of time. He'd found out all he could and had only done that as a favor. Knowing that Crankcase might be innocent didn't help in getting him off, but it did make me feel better and justified Don Ed's hunch.

CHAPTER 32

The reporter from the *Dallas Morning News* showed up again. He was at the convenience store talking to Speedy, and that was bad news.

Speedy was the best shot in the sheriff's office. He could hit anything with a pistol, rifle, or shotgun. He had great eyes, quick reflexes, and steady hands. Speedy frequently went quail hunting and killed a dozen quail with a dozen shells, shooting a little double-barrel, 410-gauge shotgun, while others banged away at the sky with 20- or even 12-gauge guns. He would double out of almost every covey and made hitting the erratic, fast-flying birds look simple. Just as skillful with a rifle, the stories of the long and difficult shots made while deer and elk hunting were legendary. Unfortunately, Speedy had one flaw—he was dumb. He had trouble filling out routine reports and was worthless when it came to any kind of complicated task. The other deputies constantly played jokes on him, taking advantage of his oblivious nature. The sheriff kept him on because he was likeable and had repeatedly won the state pistol shooting championship, competing against other law enforcement officers from across the state. Sheriff Checker said Speedy would be useful if we needed a sniper, which, of course, in Washita County, we never did.

The reporter was sporting a wide grin and the same wrinkled suit. He acted way too friendly to be trusted.

"Pleased to see you again, Deputy. Speedy and I were just discussing that standoff your Department has with Morford and the other freemen out at his farm. Speedy was telling me he knows the sheriff won't try to arrest Morford soon, because he's afraid of a violent confrontation. What's your take on that situation?" he said as he swallowed a big gulp from his fountain drink.

I noticed Speedy also had a Big Gulp cup and a candy bar. I wondered if that was cheaper than the beer the reporter offered to Red and me for information.

"Look, I told you before, talk to the sheriff. He's the boss. You're not going to get any information from me. Got it this time?"

The reporter turned to Speedy, for my benefit, and said, "Thank you, Speedy, for helping with information about the sheriff's plan. Like I said, expect to see your picture in the Dallas paper soon."

The reporter then turned and left the store, looking like a small child who had just pulled off some forbidden mischief and gotten away with it.

"Why were you talking to that weasel, Speedy? You know the sheriff told us not to talk to media."

"Well, Snake, I just answered a few questions. How could that hurt anything?"

"Speedy, politics is tricky business. How these reporters treat something can make a lot of difference. What did he want to know?"

"Just about Lucas and Morford. He acted like he already knew most of what I told him."

"Just do what the sheriff orders. These reporters will put words in your mouth and then quote you for a story."

"He took my picture, Snake. He said it would be in the Dallas paper."

"You'd better tell the sheriff, Speedy, before he sees it, or he'll be mad as hell."

"Okay. I almost forgot, but he wanted to know who Lucas was and about the bank. I told him about your dad."

"What else did you tell the reporter, Speedy?"

"Oh, just about the sheriff and stuff about the farm. I think Morford got the shaft."

"We aren't paid to talk about that, Speedy. Keep your mouth shut."

"Don't get pissy with me, Snake. I saw you and Red talking to him."

"Yes, but Red didn't know what he wanted, and I wouldn't answer his questions. Don't forget these guys from the press are weasels. They'll sensationalize anything."

A few days later I picked up the Dallas paper, and sure enough, there was a story on what the paper was now calling the "Oklahoma Standoff." The whole article was slanted so that Morford was an underdog and a hero. Lucas was rich and evil, and the sheriff's department was just a pawn for doing Lucas' dirty work. What was worse than the article was the picture showing Speedy holding a high-powered rifle and describing him as a "sniper" ready to "take out" any designated target, presumably Morford or the other freemen. Speedy looked like something out of Afghanistan or Chechnya, not western Oklahoma. Everything that the press did was making this a tougher political case for the sheriff.

CHAPTER 33

My lawyer friend had reviewed the lease on Dawn's property. As usual, Lucas was overreaching. There were still three months to run on the lease, and Dawn did not have to vacate the property immediately. Unfortunately, this wasn't much help, but at least gave her time to find another way to make a living before she had to close down the store.

I wasn't happy about having to tell her the news, but felt obligated to personally deliver the message. Coming into town, I glanced at the property I had seen before that looked like an old filling station, and like some cartoon character, a light bulb went off above my head.

At Dawn's store, she greeted me with a pleasant smile, and I could tell that she was expecting me to help her.

"I've got good news and I've got bad news, which do you want first?" I stated.

"Give me the bad news first," Dawn responded.

"Lucas has the right to evict you, but you have three months to run on your lease and you don't have to leave until the lease terminates." I could see Dawn's smile fade into a crestfallen look.

"Is that just the bad news, or is it the good news, too?"

"No, not exactly. Who owns that property that looks like an old filling station down the road?"

"Mr. Weatherby. He ran it for years before they opened the Texaco on the highway and killed his business. Besides, he was ready to retire anyway. What's the point?"

"Well, why couldn't we convert that into a store?"

"I don't know who we is, pale face, but I don't have any money or credit, and that place looks like it's about to fall apart."

"We just might include me, if the deal is right. Who is Weatherby, and is he still alive?"

Dawn began to smile when she said, "Old man Weatherby is very much alive. He's an ornery old coot, but heck, I don't know. What were you thinking about?"

"Of course, the best thing would be if Weatherby would fix it up and lease it to you. The other idea would be for me to buy it from Weatherby and lease it to you. Where can we find him?"

"Oh, he's easy to find. He stays around his place and gardens, but he's sure not easy to talk to and, he's not into charity."

"Would he talk to me?"

"No, but he might talk to me. He comes in here once in a while and buys gas. He won't deal with the Texaco. I think I'm on as good a terms with him as anybody, which doesn't say much."

"Let's go see him. What the hell have you got to lose?"

"Just my store. It's fine with me. I'm about to close for lunch, anyway, and his place isn't far. Why not right now?"

"Bring your peace pipe and not your tomahawk and let's go."

"Watch your scalp, buddy. When we see Weatherby, you may need my tomahawk."

We got in my car and Dawn directed me down a country road a few miles from town. Weatherby's place was a small, well-kept house. Behind the house was an extensive garden, and Weatherby was out there riding a lawn-sized, self-propelled tractor. Dawn waved and yelled at him, and he stopped the tractor and met us halfway between the house and the garden.

Weatherby was a little, wiry fellow in his seventies with wispy, gray hair, wearing a t-shirt, dirty khaki pants, work boots, and a baseball hat. He had what appeared to be a perpetual frown on his face.

"Hello, Dawn."

"Hello, Mr. Weatherby."

"What do you want?"

"We want to talk about your property over in town."

"Who the hell is we?"

"Me and my friend, Deputy Sheriff Frasier."

Weatherby gave me a hard look and then turned back to Dawn. "Talk."

"We would like to see about buying your property," I interjected.

Weatherby never changed his gaze from Dawn to me. "Not for sale."

"Not at any price or terms?" I asked.

"Can't you hear, son? I said, not for sale."

"Would you lease the property?"

Weatherby paused for a long time and then said, "To who?"

"To me," I said.

"No."

"To Dawn?"

There was a long pause and then Weatherby replied, "Yes."

Dawn then interjected, "Mr. Weatherby, I pay five hundred dollars a month rent where I am. That's all I can pay and still make a living. Would you lease me the property for five hundred dollars a month?"

Weatherby paused again and then said, "As is, five hundred dollars per month."

"I would like to move in three months from now, is that all right?"

"Yes."

"Good."

"What about a lease and terms?" I said.

Weatherby again looked at Dawn and said, "You fix it up."

"But what are the other terms to the lease?" I said.

Weatherby finally looked at me and pointedly said, "Good-bye," as he turned his back and walked back to his tractor. Dawn and I went to the car. When we got in and started to drive away, I couldn't help but breakdown laughing. She started to laugh, too.

"Well, I guess we got a deal," I said. "But I'm not quite sure what it is."

She looked at me, still laughing. "What do I do now?"

"Well, you, me, and Alonzo need to go to work on that property so you can move in three months. It may look like a dump, but I bet the three of us can fix it up so you can operate a store."

"What do you get out of it, Snake?"

"I get to help a friend and hurt an enemy. I don't have much to do in my spare time, anyway, but no working on Thursday nights. Alonzo and I have to play basketball on Thursday. Oh, and by the way, I want free beer every time I work on your new store."

Dawn leaned across the car and gave me a big hug. It appeared that was about as much pay as I could expect.

CHAPTER 34

It was Thursday night, so I was in Weatherford for the weekly basketball game. We were warming up at one end of the floor when Mike said, "The Ringer is here."

I looked up the floor and saw the player we called the "Ringer" warming up with the coaches. The Ringer was about six feet, six inches tall and weighed at least 240 pounds. He reminded me of Dennis Rodman without the body piercing and dyed hair. He had played college basketball at Tulsa University, and later for a year or two in the Continental Basketball Association. He was way too good for our game, but was the nephew of one of the coaches and had showed up a few weeks ago while visiting his uncle. He was big, strong, talented, and almost unstoppable in our game.

The first time the Ringer showed up, we all agreed I would have to try and guard him, even though I was giving away about three inches and forty pounds. Our tallest player was the geek graduate student, who would have no chance of keeping up with the Ringer. The first time he got the ball, I sat up on defense in front of him. He looked at me and said, "Sheriff, I'm goin' wear your white ass out," and he did. He was too good. I could overguard him inside and force him outside, in which case he would simply pop straight up and hit a long jump shot, or I could overguard him outside, in which case he'd juke one way or the other, drive past me before I could react, and score a lay-up or a dunk. Since he did occasionally miss a jump shot, I guarded him close inside, which led to constant pushing, shoving, fouling, and fights over the ball on rebounds. The Ringer caused the game to degenerate into a runaway for the coaches' team. That is, until we found the Ringer's weakness.

We discovered his weakness by accident. After Mike came down with one of his few rebounds, he started down the court and looking at the Ringer said, "Boy, you smell like shit." The Ringer went nuts. He went after Mike with a roundhouse punch. Fortunately Mike ducked and danced away. The Ringer's uncle grabbed him and held him until he cooled down, but he couldn't be calmed down enough to finish the game, and stormed off the court, muttering to himself.

The next time he showed up, I talked to his uncle and told him we weren't willing to play if he couldn't control his nephew. We came for fun, not for fighting. The uncle assured me he had talked to the Ringer and he would keep his temper. Of course, I immediately told Mike to needle the Ringer to see what would happen. At first the strategy didn't seem to be working, but finally as Mike got more and more personal, the Ringer got so mad his concentration was ruined. He threw away passes, missed easy shots, and generally reduced his game down to our level of play. We figured we'd never see the Ringer again, so I was surprised to see him warming up with the coaches. His uncle must have used some serious persuasion to get him to play. I was glad Mike was there, as our only defense was his mouth.

After the game started, Mike immediately began his insulting trash talk. The Ringer seemed to pay no attention and hit from everywhere, dominating the game to an even greater extent than he had the first time he played. After we took a rest break, Mike redoubled his efforts, but the Ringer just kept pouring in shots, grabbing rebounds, and feeding his teammates for easy shots. What was usually a close game with the coaches turned into a rout.

After the game I was leaving the gym with the Ringer's uncle and commented that his nephew had behaved himself and had, as predicted on his first outing, kicked our asses. The coach got a big smile on his face and said, "Well, Snake, I used a little strategy myself. I don't believe my nephew ever heard a word Mike said."

"You mean his concentration was that good?"

"No, I mean the ear plugs I made him wear worked that good," the coach said as he laughed uproariously. "I know he's way too good for this game, and I won't bring him back, but I couldn't let you dumb jocks out-coach me, even at pickup basketball."

CHAPTER 35

Don Ed wanted a report on my progress, or lack thereof, in finding his witness. He may have looked laid-back, but underneath his calm facade he was obsessive and compulsive. He worried every problem like a dog with a bone until he reached a solution.

Furthermore, he was clearly irritated at the bad lawyering he had just had to put up with in his courtroom. Don Ed liked lawyers and would cut them some slack when it didn't affect their client's case, but he expected everyone who appeared in his court to be prepared and ready to represent their client.

"You know, Snake, when I practiced law, I never had time to procrastinate or bullshit. I was just too damn busy. I can't stand lawyers who are dilatory. I don't understand how they can even make a living. Some lawyers don't even return their phone calls. I don't see how they stay in business. These two idiots I just had in my courtroom shouldn't even be allowed to practice. As one of my old law school professors would say, 'They may be members of the bar, but they sure as hell aren't lawyers.' Now, tell me what you've got on Crankcase's witness."

"Don Ed, I haven't been able to locate the witness. In fact, I don't even have a decent lead. I'd go further than that—I don't even have a whiff of a lead. It seems to me that the odds are stacked against Crankcase."

"Snake, you've been around long enough to know that life is not a square game. I didn't invite you up here to bitch about the problems you have in completing this assignment. I never told you it would be easy. Your problem is you've prejudged your client.

You've decided he's not worth saving. You've figured out all of the approaches that don't work. I trust you'll find a new approach that does. Crankcase's trial will be set soon. If you need more time to work on the case, I'll talk to the sheriff and see that your duties don't interfere with this assignment."

"Don Ed, you're my friend. As a friend, I'm doing this for you. But make no mistake, I don't believe Crankcase, and I don't think he's worth saving. I didn't come in here to bitch, and I sure as hell didn't come in here to take shit off some sanctimonious, middle-aged cowboy."

Don Ed gave me a stern judicial look, as though he was about to launch into another lawyerlike speech, and then he cracked a big grin.

"You know, Snake, people will take about as much shit as I'm willing to give as a judge, but I guess I reached your limit. Here's what I want you to do next. Go down to Oklahoma City and get a list of the trial exhibits and a copy of the transcript of the trial from the public defender's office. I want to look those over again. Maybe I missed something. Then, by God, go out and find that witness."

I tried to continue to look irritated, but I couldn't stay mad at Don Ed for long, and immediately started dreaming up new angles that might help me find the elusive Angel.

CHAPTER 36

A few days later I drove to Oklahoma City to pick up the records Don Ed wanted and talk to a vice-detective who was an old friend of Sheriff Checker's. The sheriff had called him in advance and asked him to talk to me as a favor. The detective had been on the police force for over twenty years, and I thought he might have some information about Angel. As it turned out he'd never heard of Angel, although he knew hundreds of young women who might fit her description. He wasn't enthusiastic about giving out information that might help Crankcase, who he thought was lower than dirt, but he did begrudgingly admit that he'd never heard of Crankcase carrying a weapon and had doubts about Crankcase's guilt, even though he was glad to have another dealer off the street.

After my meeting at the Oklahoma City Police Department, I was scheduled to meet Mike and his new girlfriend for lunch at the Lido, a Vietnamese restaurant near downtown Oklahoma City. Oddly enough, Oklahoma City had a thriving and sizable Vietnamese community. After the fall of Saigon, a large number of Vietnamese refugees were housed at Ft. Chaffee Army Base in Arkansas. General Clyde Watts, a reserve U.S. Army general who had served in China during World War II; his son, Charles, who was an Army officer in Vietnam; and Ellis Edwards, another Vietnam veteran who later became state treasurer, were instrumental in relocating a large number of those refugees to the Oklahoma City area.

At the time it was a controversial subject. Some provincial and jingoistic Oklahoma City citizens were opposed to having foreigners move into the community. However, as time passed, Watts was proven correct in his assessment of the Vietnamese, who became some of the best citizens in the community. Typically the Vietnamese refugees were industrious, family oriented, and ambitious. They started businesses, rejuvenated older neighborhoods, and their children became successful students who thrived in the public school system. Basically they were solid citizens, taxpayers, and entrepreneurs.

The Vietnamese community had developed a wide range of businesses around NW 23rd Street and Classen in Oklahoma City. Restaurants, groceries, tailor shops, and a few professional and service businesses all flourished in the area, now known as the Asian District. One of the popular Vietnamese restaurants was the Lido, which was always crowded at lunch.

Mike and his new girlfriend had already been seated when I arrived. Mike had warned me that she did not want to be identified as Lucas' daughter, and that I should not mention the connection. The waiter seated me at the table and Mike introduced her as Butterfly.

"Excuse me, but is your name really Butterfly?"

"Yes, that's my legal name. I had it changed. I saw a beautiful butterfly flying on a perfect spring day, and I knew that my karma required me to change my name. Ever since I adopted the name, my life has changed for the better."

"Don't you think it's sort of ironic that you've taken up with a crop duster who kills insects for a living?"

"I've been trying to forgive Mike for that. He takes me in his airplane and we fly like butterflies. It's wonderful."

"He tells me he could fly better if he had a jet," I responded, causing Mike to shoot me a dirty look.

Butterfly was pretty, in an angular sort of way. She was thin, with short-cut hair and severe, almost gaunt features. Mike told me she was clean, but her eyes had that unfocused, crazy look that is usually associated with drugs. She was dressed in a long-sleeve T-shirt, dark red, velvet pants, and boots, set off by gold bracelets, rings, and earrings. When the waitress came to take our order, she ordered only vegetarian dishes and made a point of telling me she was a strict vegetarian.

"Did you find out anything about the missing witness?" Mike asked.

"Not a damn thing. If it weren't for Don Ed, I'd give up on this whole project. I'm afraid it's a wild goose chase."

Mike mentioned that I'd gone to school at Stanford, which provoked Butterfly to begin a conversation about Berkley, San Francisco, and the Bay area. It seems her daddy had sent her to school at Mills College in Oakland. She didn't last long there, and took off with a bunch of other deadheads, ending up living in San Francisco. We compared notes about San Francisco, but it turned out she was so stoned most of the time she lived there that she didn't have much information of interest. She and her friends had moved on to Los Angeles after a few months, and later she had aimlessly drifted back to Oklahoma City.

As I listened to Butterfly talk and watched her actions, there was something that bothered me about her. I couldn't quite place my uneasiness. It was as if I'd know her before, even though I was sure I'd never met her. It might have been her wild eyes, or her erratic way of jumping from one subject to another, with no explanation. In any event, there was an air about her that didn't seem right, but did seem familiar. Whatever it was about Butterfly that bothered me certainly didn't affect Mike. He clearly thought she was wonderful. He laughed at all of her jokes and pretended to understand her comments, no matter how obscure and spacey.

After lunch, Mike and I were standing outside the restaurant waiting for Butterfly to go to the restroom.

"This is finally the one, Snake. I can't imagine that I've found someone who's as pretty and smart as Butterfly."

"And as crazy as you are, Mike."

"That, too. We're compatible in that respect."

"Mike, I hate to ask this, but is she on something?"

"Only a prescription her psychiatrist gave her. I think it's something like Prozac. She won't even touch a beer. She's been clean for over two years. I care so much about her I don't even smoke grass when she's around."

"I hope it works out for you, Mike. I'd like to ride in a jet, especially one that I knew was paid for by Lucas."

"You're all heart, Snake. I'll try to keep that in mind when I'm enjoying my early retirement."

Butterfly came out of the restaurant and joined us where we were standing next to Mike's car.

"I think I knew you in a prior life, Snake. I recognize your aura. It's friendly, and I know that I'll see you again."

"I promised to take Butterfly flying this afternoon, Snake, so we have to go. Keep in touch," Mike said. As they got into his car to leave, Butterfly gave me a kiss on the cheek.

On the way back to Cordell, I pondered where I'd seen Butterfly before and what made her seem familiar. It sure as hell wasn't in another life, since I'd only had one so far, and that was plenty.

CHAPTER 37

I was changing into my running clothes and watching the six o'clock news on TV when Mike called, as usual at an inconvenient time.

"This is the sheriff over in Beckham County. I'm holding your friend Michael O' Connell on 103 counts of bad behavior. He wants you to come over and put up his bail."

"Tell him I wouldn't piss on the best part of him if he was on fire, but if he wants to buy me a beer, I might negotiate.

I glanced at the TV and was surprised to see the sheriff. He was standing in front of the courthouse facing a talking-head reporter. Sheriff Checker looked uncomfortable.

"Mike, turn on channel nine, quick. The sheriff is being interrogated. I'll call you back."

The reporter tried to goad the sheriff into some remark he might regret, but although it was easy to tell Chubby was angry, he pretty much kept his cool. The problem was, he didn't have a solution for the standoff and it was obvious. That pleased the reporter, as he could see an ongoing story that could continue to be sensationalized.

The phone rang again. It was Mike calling back.

"Let's attack from the sky. I'll rent a helicopter and we'll hit the militia when they're not expecting it and take them by surprise. I'll fly, and you can get your first taste of combat."

"I'm glad you're a pilot and not a sheriff, Mike. Meet me for a beer and we'll discuss tactics—hoop tactics. I can help you with that."

"No guts, no glory," Mike said as he abruptly hung up the phone.

CHAPTER 38

R ed may not seem too smart to people who didn't know him well. He had a high school education, but never went to college, and as far as I knew, didn't read anything but the sports page in the newspaper. Red was certainly no intellectual, but he was clever in that deceptive, country way that fools a lot of people, especially those with a preconceived notion of small-town folks. Red might talk like a hick, but he damn sure didn't think like one, and he knew his job.

Red was coming out of the Dairy Queen with his favorite chocolate milkshake when he saw the truck and the two strangers who had met us at the gate to Morford's place. The truck had Idaho plates and was rattling through town in the direction of Morford's farm.

Red called in to check on the plates, but the truck wasn't stolen and belonged to an Idaho resident. He followed the strangers anyway, staying well back past the end of town. Sure enough, when they reached the county road to Morford's farm, the drivers gunned the truck way past the speed limit, and Red hit his red light and siren and closed on them fast from behind.

The truck pulled over on the shoulder, and Red approached on foot from behind, ordering the occupants to stay in the cab. As he passed the bed of the truck he noticed a large piece of green canvas pulled over the top of what appeared to be a good-sized crate or trunk. He might have never learned what was under the canvas if the driver hadn't been armed.

When Red asked the driver for his license, he immediately saw the big, army 45 caliber automatic strapped to his hip. The passenger also had a .38 stuck in his belt. They both said they were licensed to carry, but while Red ran a check he made them get out and took their side arms. He then called for backup, and in just a few minutes Speedy and Lookout roared up in another sheriff's vehicle.

Red thought he had legal grounds to search the truck because the men were armed, so he did. Under the canvas he found a wooden crate marked U.S. Army. He pried open the crate, which revealed its contents—a rocket launcher and a dozen rockets.

The deputies then brought the truck's occupants and the truck and its contents into town. The men were held for questioning and the DA was called. Unfortunately, Sherman had trained his troops well. Neither one would give more than their name and address. The driver was the owner of the truck and they were both licensed to carry weapons. Neither man had a felony record, but after inquiry through the U.S. district attorney's office in Oklahoma City, the contents of the crate were identified as stolen from the National Guard armory in Arkansas. The men were then turned over to the feds and Speedy and Lookout took them down to Oklahoma City, pending federal charges.

The DA wasn't sure if this helped us to take action against Sherman or Morford, but it sure cut down on the freemen's firepower if we had to take them on with force.

The sheriff offered Red a bonus, another chocolate milkshake, since the one he had in the car had melted before he could drink the whole thing.

CHAPTER 39

The sheriff told me Floyd had filed a motion on behalf of the bank requesting a writ of assistance ordering the sheriff to remove Morford from his farm. The motion was scheduled to be heard right away, and if it was granted, the sheriff would be in one hell of a bind. So I dropped by to see Don Ed.

Don Ed was in an expansive mood and wanted to talk. I always knew when he had something on his mind and wanted to use me as an audience.

"Look, Snake, I know how you feel about Lucas and Sherman, and you're justified. But you don't hate a person because you disagree with their ideas. You hate a person because he's an asshole. I don't hate you or Chubby even though you are for the death penalty. You're my friends. I didn't hate the prosecutors who were on the other side of my capital cases, even though I totally disagreed with what they were doing. They were as committed to their ideas as I was to mine. Of course, there were one or two who were assholes. I hated them because they were assholes, not because they were prosecutors seeking the death penalty."

"The same is true of political ideas. Look at the Kennedys and the Rockefellers. A lot of people hated them because of their so-called liberal views. On the other hand, they could have been totally worthless, rich dilettantes instead of being productive citizens, dedicating themselves to public service. That doesn't mean you can't hate Teddy Kennedy because he acted recklessly and cowardly at Chappaquiddick, or you can't like Jack Kennedy because he acted bravely as the Captain of PT 109."

"I don't understand these one-issue zealots that despise everyone who disagrees with their ideas. That's pure bigotry. The worst are the ones who invoke God and Jesus as the ultimate authority for their position. The greatest injustices in the world have been committed in the name of religion."

"The anti-abortion crowd is some of the worst. I had to rule on a case where the parents wanted an injunction to keep their daughter from having an abortion. The law was clearly in favor of the pregnant daughter. I threw the parents' case out of court. Two days later I got a postcard from the parents. It was a drawing of a tombstone with the words 'RIP this child was killed by Judge Roberts.' The same people are probably for the death penalty. I can live with that, but what I can't stand is them trying to run other people's lives."

"Now Lucas is a person we can all hate. He is a greedy, moneygrubbing, heartless, worthless, son of a bitch. On the other hand, there is no reason to hate Morford or maybe even some of those other people that are out at Morford's place. They don't like or trust the government. That's their position, and it's not without cause. Sherman's another story. He's in it for himself. You told me he's a mercenary, and that comes as no surprise. He just uses people like Morford for his own purposes. Come to think of it, that means we have a son of a bitch on both sides of this matter."

"Even though I probably tend to agree with Sherman's view of the government, I am now part of government, at least the state government, and at some point I am going to have to issue a writ of assistance mandating the sheriff to enforce the judgment. Why don't you tell Chubby to do his best to get this problem solved, and I'll delay the bank's motion for a few weeks, even though it will cause Floyd a lot of grief from his client, which he doesn't really deserve."

"Thanks, Judge. I have faith in Chubby, but I'm worried about how he'll solve this mess."

"Snake, I'm not concerned about Chubby. He'll do what has to be done in the end. Some people talk tough, and some people are tough. Chubby is tough. He doesn't have to brag or bully to hide a weakness. He'll get the job done."

"I agree, but I worry that whatever he does may cost him too much politically."

"That's a problem, but not so much in a county this small. Just about everybody knows he's going to have to make a decision and live with it, and most folks will cut him a little slack.

"I hope you're right, Judge."

"As far as Crankcase's witness is concerned, I suggest you go see Crapshooter."

"Why Crapshooter? He's no criminal lawyer."

"Politics, that's why. He's so tight with the DA he can get almost anything he wants out of that office. Maybe there's someone in the DA's office that knows something about your lost witness."

"I thought they had to open up their files to the defendant these days. Besides, why would they help Crankcase?"

"First of all, I didn't say there would be anything in the file. They don't have any obligation to look for exonerating witnesses that may not even exist, but that doesn't mean they don't have information that never gets documented or turned over to the defense."

"So what? I still don't think they would help Crankcase."

"You don't get it, Snake. That's not what it's about. It's the old political game. Reward your friends and punish your enemies. Crapshooter raises a hundred grand every time the DA runs for re-election. If Crapshooter wants a favor for a buddy or a client, and it doesn't cause the DA a problem, then the DA delivers on the favor. Trust me and go see Crapshooter."

So that's what I did.

CHAPTER 40

Crapshooter was a big-time lawyer in Oklahoma City whose real name was Jim Rendell. He claimed to know the inside scoop on everything that went on, whether politics, business, sports, or law, and Don Ed's encouragement to see him seemed well-founded. Crapshooter might be able to pick up some information from the DA's office regarding the first trial or Crankcase's pathetic defense counsel.

Almost everyone in the legal community called Rendell Crapshooter, a name he earned because he was a gambler in every way. He was willing to take big chances on cases other lawyers had refused. As a result of his style, he enjoyed both spectacular failures and successes. He loved to have the odds against him and was always able to reconcile losing by blaming bad luck, prejudiced judges, or misguided juries. Crapshooter never doubted his ability, and his ego was legendary.

Crapshooter's office was, of course, huge and absurdly ornate. It had been designed by an interior decorator he flew in from California. There were so many expensive paintings, sculptures, and just "things" around his office that it had a confusing and disoriented type of appearance.

After a brief wait in Crapshooter's reception room, where I was served coffee from an expensive China cup by a well-dressed receptionist, I was ushered in to see the great man himself. I knew Crapshooter from serving process for him in western Oklahoma. He loved to sue oil companies and had used me to serve papers in a number of cases. As usual, he was dressed in an impeccably tailored, dark suit with a patterned tie that no doubt was a Versace or Armani. Crapshooter was tall and thin with an angular face set off by a thin, black moustache. He fancied himself handsome, but he always looked just a little too slick. He might dress up in a fancy way, but it was hard to cover his greedy heart.

"Always good to see you, Snake. What can I help you with?"

"I'm trying to help Don Ed find a witness who might be instrumental in the defense of Crankcase's murder trial. I wonder if you have heard anything about the first trial from either the prosecutor or Crankcase's lawyer, or maybe even just courthouse gossip that might be useful in locating the witness."

"Of course, I do know just about everything that's going on at the courthouse, and I've got a direct line into the DA's office. I don't know anything now, but I would be glad to check with my sources. I was just getting ready to fly out to Palm Springs with my buddy, the ex-president of Shell Oil Company, to play some golf. When I get back, I'll make a few calls and let you know. Check with my secretary on the way out I think we have some more subpoenas to serve out in your part of the country."

"Thanks for your help," I said and rose to leave.

Crapshooter stopped me and remarked, "Snake, answer me something. Here you are a graduate of Stanford with a background in banking and a good way with people. What in the hell are you doing in that hick town, serving process and guarding the jail? I could get you a job in a bank in Oklahoma City or Dallas with one phone call. You could start as a vice president and make four times what you make out there. I would be glad to help you."

"I appreciate the offer, and don't think I haven't thought about it since I got back to Oklahoma, but I'm comfortable with where I am and what I am, just like you are with what you do. But thanks anyway."

"Suit yourself. But when you change your mind, the offer's open."

A few weeks later I got a call from Crapshooter's secretary (the great man never placed his own calls, he was far too important for that). She asked me to hold for Mr. Rendell, who came on the line and stated, "Snake, I don't have much for you, but here's what I know. Even the prosecutor has doubts about whether Crankcase committed this murder. He had no reputation for violence or carrying weapons. He was small-time. There's some talk that the taxi driver was taken out by a much bigger fish than Crankcase. As far as this witness you keep talking about, the DA doesn't believe she exists, and even the defense lawyer didn't buy Crankcase's story, although he's so lazy he probably wouldn't have looked for the witness anyway. I'm not sure what you do next, but Don Ed will surely know. If I were you, I would keep digging. Your client may not be worth saving, but he may be innocent of this crime."

"Thanks for the information. By the way, how did you come out in that golf game with that big executive?"

"He's such a hacker; I almost hate to play with him. Worse yet, he insists on a stroke a hole. He likes to play me in the winter or early spring when he's been out at Palm Springs every day playing and I've been back here in snow and ice practicing law. What that all means is I beat him by fifteen shots and still lost a thousand dollars. I'll get him next time."

CHAPTER 41

It wasn't long before I was back in Burns Flat. Dawn had gotten a key to the old filling station from Weatherby. Alonzo was there, and the three of us went down to look at her new emporium. It was a dump. The structure wasn't too bad, and the roof looked like it could be repaired, but the place had been empty for five to six years, and the interior was mostly mice droppings, spider webs, and trash left by a homeless person who had lived in the building.

Alonzo and I went to work on the roof first. We decided to replace the whole roof with asphalt tiles. It was hot, tiresome work in the Oklahoma sun, but it was the kind of work that had a beginning and an end. You could see the results, unlike looking for a probably non-existent witness. There was satisfaction in just seeing the roof finished.

After the roof, we replaced all of the windows. I had five thumbs when it came to carpentry, and Alonzo wasn't much better, but fortunately Dawn proved handy as a carpenter and the windows fit well enough. I had to put the bill for the materials on my credit card. I told Dawn it was a loan. I'd collect later when she could pay. This time I got a kiss and a hug. She also came through with a cold six-pack at the end of each job. At least my pay was improving.

Securing the roof and windows took us a month, with most of the work done on Saturdays and Sundays. We'd already used up a lot of the time left on Dawn's lease, but since we could work inside now, we could start working nights to finish. It would be close, but I thought we could still finish before Dawn's lease ran out.

We cleaned up the inside, rebuilt the counter, and had another friend of Dawn's, who was a real handyman, checked the plumbing and electrical. The electrical was old and had to be replaced, and the plumbing was not great, but with a little work, still functioned. The friend found an old gas heater somewhere and installed it in what used to be the garage part of the station. Dawn's suppliers helped and put in a freezer and a big cooler for the ice cream, beer, pop, and other items that required refrigeration. Dawn would have to use window air conditioners, but the place was beginning to look serviceable.

Everything seemed to be working, until we started to get ready to sell gasoline. The old tanks had been removed by the Corporation Commission for environmental purposes. The oil companies all wanted some kind of deposit or financial guarantee and a security bond before they would install new tanks and pumps.

I had a small savings and had been putting away money in a mutual fund, but wasn't in a position to help Dawn anymore financially. Things were going well, but if she couldn't sell gasoline it was going to be impossible to compete with whomever Lucas got to take over her old location. We were stumped.

We hadn't seen Weatherby since we started work on the property. Then one night about eight o'clock he walked into the old filling station, unannounced. He was dressed as usual in khaki pants but this time with a long-sleeve khaki shirt and a straw cowboy hat. Without saying a word, he walked around looking at the store, then walked outside, circled the building, and returned.

"Thank you for letting me lease the building, Mr. Weatherby," Dawn said.

"How are things?" Weatherby replied.

"Good, Mr. Weatherby…but there is one problem."

"What?"

"The oil companies won't put in the pumps or the tanks without some kind of money or credit, and that I don't have. I can't compete with Lucas' store if I don't sell gas."

"That it?" Weatherby replied.

"Well, I guess everything else is fine, except for the gasoline sales…"

"I'll take care of it for two cents a gallon," Weatherby said.

"How about one cent?" I replied.

"Are you deaf, son? I said two cents," Weatherby retorted as he turned and walked out of the building, leaving all of us laughing and shaking our heads.

"The man said two cents. I think I heard him," I said, which brought on another round of relieved laughter.

The next thing we heard was a call from a local gasoline distributor in Clinton. He asked Dawn when she wanted the pumps and tanks installed, and soon trucks pulled up to the store and began digging holes for the tanks, and then the pumps were installed and the entire area in the front of the store asphalted. We didn't hear a word from Weatherby and had no idea what arrangement he'd made with the gasoline distributor, but the store was now ready to open for business.

After the pumps were installed, the word around town was that Lucas was having a hard time finding anyone to take over the old property.

"It couldn't happen to a nicer guy," was my response.

CHAPTER 42

The next Friday was the grand opening of Dawn's store. Everything was in place, even the neon beer signs in the windows, so on Thursday night we decided to celebrate. Red, Mike, and the district attorney, who had looked at the lease for Dawn, came over to Burns Flat and all of Dawn's family was there for the celebration. There were so many Indians it looked more like a powwow than a store opening.

Little kids ran in and out of the store laughing, chasing each other, wrestling, and generally having fun. Two teenagers threw a Frisbee back and forth in the parking lot, and a crowd of locals moved in and out of the store, talking with each other and congratulating Dawn.

Dawn gave out free beer, pop, and ice cream. Alonzo and I basked in our glory as head carpenters, while Mike and Red drank beer and stared at the young Native American girls. The DA just kept shaking his head and saying, "I can't believe this. It's my best case this year."

Dawn told me she had invited Weatherby.

"What did he say?"

"No," she replied.

"How about Lucas? Dawn, you should have invited him to see his competition."

"Maybe he's over in the other store, but since it's dark and he hasn't found anyone to lease it, I doubt it."

About eight o'clock Dawn whistled for silence. "Listen up, everybody. I want to thank Alonzo and Snake for all their help. I couldn't have done it without them."

She turned then and pulled out two boxes, handing one to Alonzo and one to me.

"Here's a present for all your help, guys. Open them so the folks can see."

Alonzo and I tore open our boxes to each disclose a brand new hammer. That got a laugh out of the crowd. I brandished mine above my head like a war club, showing off like a kid. Everyone was in such a good mood that I got another laugh.

Dawn yelled for silence again.

"I've asked my uncle to bless this place with a Kiowa prayer. Uncle, take it away."

A big, heavyset man dressed in complete Native American costume, including a brightly colored feather headdress, stepped forward. He was swinging a smoking urn from side to side and began to chant and move his feet in rhythm, creating a slow dance that seemed to follow his chant. At the end of the ceremony he placed a necklace around Dawn's neck and stepped back. Dawn's eyes glistened as she said, "The ceremony means this place is a blessed place for the Kiowas and safe from their enemies."

"I guess that means Lucas," I said, which brought on another laugh.

The party began to wind down, and I hugged Dawn and headed for my car. As I left town, I glanced at Lucas' darkened property and the cheery crowd leaving Dawn's. For the first time in years, I felt like I had a family and someone to care about. It was a good feeling.

CHAPTER 43

The store may have been finished, but I wasn't finished with Dawn. It must have been her eyes, because that's what I always remembered. She had laughing eyes, dark brown and hard to forget. So I called and asked her to go to dinner in Clinton.

"You mean a real date? I haven't been out on a date since high school," she chuckled. "Sure, Snake, I'll go. I kind of miss your bad jokes."

"I'll try to improve my repertoire. That's a big word I learned in college. I hope you are impressed."

"At least not depressed. I'll get a babysitter for Friday night."

We went to dinner and joked and laughed about Lucas and Old Man Weatherby. She told me stories about Alonzo growing up, and how she had gotten married when she was eighteen because she didn't know any better. I told her about Kit, and that I was old enough to know better. I confirmed that it was definitely her eyes. She had a lithe, slim body that appealed to me, but it was her dark brown eyes that drew me to her.

We drove back to her house in Burns Flat. It was a small brick house not far from the school. She asked me in, and when we entered it reminded me of the store—neat and clean—although the presence of her son was evident in the ball, glove, and bat by the kitchen door.

We sat on the somewhat worn sofa in the living room.

"I've had fun, Snake. Thanks for the date."

"I always like being around you, Dawn."

"Even when you are painting or fixing my roof?"

"Well, don't press the point. I might have to withdraw the

always part, and that isn't going to help when I put my best move on you."

"Oh yeah, and when might that be?"

"I'd say, right about now," I replied as I pulled her to me and bent to kiss her.

This time she did not reply, but relaxed into my chest as we exchanged a deep kiss, and relaxed even more as I began to run my hands over her slim, firm body. We undressed each other and made love on her couch. She was eager and passionate. Afterward we lay together talking.

"I think you're someone I can trust, Snake. I've thought about it. You make me laugh and you helped me when I needed help."

"Me, too, Dawn. I want to be with you. You make me feel good. I want to be around, if you'll let me."

"I'll let you, but you'll have to stop chasing that crazy lady down in Oklahoma City."

"Mike talks too much, but it doesn't matter. I haven't seen her in months."

"Let's work on years."

"I prefer to start with days, but they add up pretty fast. Remember the store."

"How could I forget?"

So we talked and idled away a slow time until she had to go pick up her son. I wanted to believe I had found something worthwhile, but experience had made me cautious.

CHAPTER 44

The 911 call came in to the sheriff's department from a motorist calling on his cell phone. He had found a highway patrol trooper lying by his patrol car on the shoulder of a state road that led into the interstate near Burns Flat. The trooper was unconscious and badly beaten. The dispatcher called for an ambulance, and the sheriff himself, along with all other available deputies, headed out for the scene.

Red and I arrived at about the same time as the ambulance. The trooper was still on the ground and still unconscious. He lay at an odd angle on the shoulder of the highway a short distance in front of his car. There was blood all over his head, face, and shirt, and his left arm looked like it was broken. His gun was still in its holster. He was in bad shape but still alive.

The paramedics began to work on him and then got him onto a stretcher and into the ambulance, leaving the scene for the Clinton hospital, the nearest emergency room.

There were tracks on the shoulder of another vehicle, which apparently had been parked in front of the patrol car. It looked like whatever happened had occurred as a result of a traffic stop. The hood of the patrol car was still warm, and the motorist who reported the incident thought he had seen some kind of SUV pulling onto the road as he approached the patrol car from behind. He called 911 immediately on his cell phone and reported the problem, so the incident must have happened only shortly before he arrived at the scene.

We secured the area to preserve the tire tracks of the other vehicle and any other physical evidence we might find. The sheriff had already called the highway patrol, who said they would send out a forensic expert from Oklahoma City. The only other evidence we could find in a search of the scene was what may have been a faint footprint near where the patrolman had been found. If the patrolman made it, he could identify the attacker. Otherwise, it was going to be hard to catch the perpetrator, particularly if he was a transient just passing through the county.

On the way back to town, Red and I discussed the case. For some reason, we both felt it was tied to Sherman. Maybe it was just because we had him on our minds, or maybe it was a premonition of some kind.

CHAPTER 45

The highway patrol and OSBI scoured the scene of the attack, but found little useful evidence. It looked like it was going to be up to the patrolman to identify his attackers, if he recovered from the beating he'd taken. He was in intensive care and still unconscious after twenty-four hours, suffering from a severe concussion, four broken ribs, a broken arm, and internal injuries.

The OSBI showed the witness pictures of SUVs, but he couldn't identify the make, model, or even the color of the vehicle he had seen. Due to the rural area where the attack had occurred, no one else had seen what happened. The incident was widely publicized on TV and in the local press, and any passerby who might have seen the other vehicle, or its occupant, was urged to contact law enforcement authorities, but no one offered any information.

After almost two days, the patrolman regained consciousness, but still remained weak and incoherent. In any event, after so much time had passed, the perpetrator was no doubt long gone.

Finally, after another day, the patrolman was able to talk. He described an attack by two men, whom he had stopped for speeding. He had approached the driver's side of the vehicle and asked for the driver's license. As the driver extended a license through the window, the passenger had exited the car. The patrolman ordered the passenger to stay in the car, but apparently was distracted long enough for the driver to throw open the door and kick the patrolman's legs out from under him. The two assailants were on top of the patrolman before he could get up or pull his weapon, kicking and stomping him into unconsciousness.

He remembered the driver had long hair and a human skull and swastika tattooed on his arm. He didn't get a good look at the passenger, but had the impression he was a big man wearing army fatigues. When shown a picture of Leland, he made a positive identification. However he could not identify a picture of Sherman as the passenger.

The information was all the sheriff needed for an assault on Morford's farm. He went immediately to the DA for a warrant for Leland's arrest and called Glenn to coordinate with the highway patrol. Glenn said he wanted to be in on the arrest, was on his way from Oklahoma City, and would bring other patrolmen to help. Glenn soon arrived along with eight other patrolmen, all armed with shotguns, rifles, and armored vests.

The sheriff and Glenn agreed to arrest Leland and take Sherman into custody for questioning. The arrests would be carried out peacefully if possible, but none of us expected either Leland or Sherman to give up without a fight.

The sheriff and Glenn huddled over a map of the area around Morford's farm, and after some discussion, agreed on a plan. The sheriff, Glenn, and the patrolmen would all proceed straight through the main gate and up the road and take a position covering the house. They would call the farmhouse when they were in place and ask Leland and Sherman to surrender. If this failed, they were prepared for an assault on the house with tear gas and whatever force was required. The deputies would be stationed around the perimeter of the farm in case Leland or Morford tried to escape across country on foot or in a four-wheel drive vehicle.

After proceeding to the farm, Red and I took our position on an adjacent country road and checked in by radio with the sheriff, who had arrived at the main gate with the troopers. Before long, we were all in place and the sheriff signaled that he was beginning the assault on Morford's house. Just a few minutes later, we were all summoned to the farm by the sheriff.

Upon answering the phone, Morford had advised the sheriff that he and Reverend Brown were the only people left at the farm and that all of his other "guests" had been gone for several days. The assault team was still suspicious and approached the farm compound with caution, but after searching the premises, found Morford's assertion true.

When we arrived at the farmhouse, the sheriff and Glen were standing in the yard questioning Morford and the Reverend Brown, both of whom denied any knowledge of where Leland, Sherman, or the others had gone.

The reverend was a portly man who affected a biblical style beard. He was dressed in jeans and suspenders and carried a bible, but not a gun, as previously advertised. He was clearly looking for a photo op and was disappointed no reporters had accompanied the assault team. However, like any good ham, he could play to any sized audience and didn't miss the chance to give us a sermon on decency and the government's interference with religious and political rights.

Under questioning from the sheriff, the reverend became more and more agitated and finally began to wave his arms and intone in a loud voice, "They go to preach it on the mountains. They go to tell it on the mountains. You'll never find them until they tell the word, pass the word, and preach the word. Leave us good people alone, and go look for the abortionists and pornographers that threaten civilization."

"Reverend, I assure you we'll find the criminals that threaten civilization, including Leland and anyone else who attacked that highway patrolman," Glenn responded.

Morford did at least identify Sherman's car as a late model Explorer with Colorado license plates. He also confirmed that both Leland and Sherman were armed and that they left together three or four days before. This was apparently all the information we were going to get.

I also used this as a chance to serve the writ of assistance on Morford ordering him off the property and causing another diatribe from the reverend. The sheriff told him if he wasn't off the property in twenty-four hours, he would be a trespasser and subject to arrest. Morford made no comment, but simply turned and disappeared into his house followed by the reverend, who was still preaching about the inequity of the system.

CHAPTER 46

I was sitting in Don Ed's reception room swapping stories with his court reporter, Judy. She was a good-looking young woman prone to wearing short, tight skirts. She had just broken the hearts of the entire western Oklahoma Bar Association by deciding to marry her high school sweetheart, a truck driver from Clinton. Don Ed finished the conference he was holding with two attorneys in his chambers, ushered me in, and offered me a seat.

"What have you got to report on my missing witness?"

"I don't have any information on the witness, but I have found information that indicates that Crankcase may not have committed the murder."

"That's very interesting. Is the evidence you've found anything that can be used in court to help in Crankcase's defense?"

"Unfortunately, no. What I learned is that 'the word on the street' is that the taxi driver was killed by a big drug dealer the driver had double-crossed on a previous drug deal. Besides, nobody ever heard of Crankcase carrying a knife or any other kind of weapon."

"That may be reassuring, Snake, but it hardly helps Crankcase or his lawyer in putting together a defense for this case. Do you think you can find the witness?"

"It's unlikely, if she exists at all."

"Well, I want you to keep trying. In the meantime, I've been thinking about this case. The original defense counsel made another mistake."

"What was that?"

"He didn't have tests run on the blood on the victim's clothing. There was blood all over the taxi driver and his clothes. Of course, most of the blood had to be from the deceased, but it's possible that someone who attacked him with a knife would have cut himself or been cut, if the driver defended himself. I have tipped off the public defender, and he's filing a motion with the court to have the bloody clothes tested to see if more than one blood type exists. If there is another blood type besides the deceased's, and it's not Crankcase's, this could be important evidence for the defense. With DNA they can go even further with the blood analysis and prove it is or isn't Crankcase's blood."

"You know, Don Ed, I don't know why you waste your time as a judge. You're one hell of a lot smarter lawyer than those damn talking heads I see on TV, like that complete asshole, Dershkowitz. You ought to be making the big bucks by at least consulting on murder cases, even if your ticker won't let you try the cases anymore."

"Thanks, Snake, but I like it fine right here. You can take the boy out of the country, but you can't take the country out of the boy. I may miss rodeoing, but I don't miss the pressure of being responsible for a defendant's life in a death penalty case. I've done more than enough of that for one lifetime."

"Well, I'll say this, Judge. Knowing that your client may be innocent does make me more interested in trying to help. Even though he's a thief, a drug dealer, and no good son of a bitch, he may not be a murderer. I'm not a lawyer, but I sure don't want to see anybody who's innocent convicted of a crime, much less executed. Furthermore, maybe the Oklahoma City Police could look for the real criminal if Crankcase gets off, even though they probably couldn't find their ass with both hands."

"Snake, you may be learning something living out here in God's country that they didn't teach you at that fancy university where your daddy sent you. By the way, you've already found out more about this case than I ever thought you could. You may make a private detective yet. Keep in touch, and I'll let you know when Crankcase's trial is scheduled to start."

"I'm not going to quit looking for the witness. A long time ago I adopted the motto 'don't never shoot short.' That came from my high school basketball coach. You probably remember what a terrible coach he was. He only lasted a couple of years before he quit and became a used car salesman. He killed the English language, and one time at practice he was angry at one of our guards who kept shooting short and hitting the front rim on his shots. He called the team together and proclaimed angrily 'don't never shoot short.' Of course, being the wise guy that I was I said, 'Coach does that mean never shoot short or always shoot short?' Since he had used the dreaded double negative, I couldn't help myself. The next thing I knew I was running fifty wind sprints and then fifty stairs. It was well worth it. I don't think I stopped laughing the whole time I was running. Of course that didn't endear me to the coach, but we had such a small school, and so few players, he had to keep playing me anyway."

"The other memorable moment of Coach's lackluster career came during halftime of his last game. We were behind as usual, and rather than give us his normal, lame attempt at a motivational speech, he decided to use the time to hand out business cards for his used car salesman job and to see if any of the players were interested in a truck or car. It was probably the best halftime speech he ever gave, as we came back in the second half and won the game, one of our rare victories. Oh, by the way, he had a teaching certificate. At least he only taught drivers ed and shop, and not English or history."

Don Ed looked at me with a quizzical smile on his face. "Well all of us need our heroes, Snake, and sometimes we find them in strange places. In any event, just keep looking, follow any leads you can think of, but don't never shoot short."

With that, Don Ed picked up a fat-looking legal brief that was sitting on this desk and began reading, a signal that the meeting was over. So I headed back to my office, after one more glance at Judy's good-looking legs.

CHAPTER 47

Since I couldn't quit, I decided to try the only other so-called lead I had found. Crankcase had told me about another drug dealer who he thought might have had the taxi driver killed. The dealer, whose name was Rhamad Asheen, had moved to Las Vegas, but one of his associates was serving time in the state prison in McAlester. The prisoner, who went by one name, Kareem, thought he was set up by Rhamad and hated Rhamad's guts. Crankcase thought Kareem might be willing to work a deal to rat out Rhamad for time off his sentence. This sounded pretty unlikely to me since finks didn't last long in prison. I figured Kareem wouldn't be making any deals, short of one that got him out of prison, which also seemed unlikely.

It took me several weeks to find the time to drive down to McAlester in the southeast part of the state. The prison there was old and grim like Granite, but at least had some grass and trees around the outside. The security was tight with metal detectors, a pat-down search, and careful checking of my ID.

When I finally was able to confront Kareem, who remained handcuffed and leg chained so the guard could leave the room, I knew almost instantly I wasn't going to get anywhere.

Kareem was a big man, well over six feet and 250 pounds, with huge, ripped arms and shoulders, sculpted by long hours pumping iron in the prison yard. He had tattoos of snakes curling up both of his arms. His expression was, at best, a glower. He radiated hate and violence.

I explained to him who I was and why I was there, while he gave me a dead-eyed, prison stare that said, you're wasting my time, you white piece of shit.

"Do you know Crankcase?"

"Asshole motha fucka."

"Do you know a man named Rhamad Asheen?"

"Asshole motha fucka."

"Did you ever deal drugs to some young, white girl named Angel?"

His response to this brought about his first change of expression, a snarling laugh.

I tried to talk to him about maybe making some kind of deal.

"See my motha fuckin' lawyer. I got nothing to say."

So it went, until I finally grew tired of wasting my time and called for the guard to let me out and return the great Kareem to the place where he belonged—for the rest of his life.

Since I had already driven so far just to waste my time talking to another criminal loser, I decided I had earned a little time off for recreation. It wasn't too much further to the Ouchita Trail. The Ouchita Trail winds through southeast Oklahoma into Arkansas, meandering through heavily wooded mountains and pine forests for over two hundred miles. It looked like a good way to spend a day would be hiking part of the trail. The weather was good, so I drove out of McAlester headed south for Poteau, the nearest town to the trail of any size.

I got into Poteau in the evening with a couple of hours of daylight left. After checking into Black Angus Motel, a decent looking, fifties-style place which was fairly clean and only moderately seedy, I still had time to climb what was advertised as "The World's Tallest Hill," 1999 feet tall, just one foot short of a mountain.

After hiking up the hill at a brisk pace, I strode and semi-jogged down just as darkness arrived. After a dinner of mediocre pizza and Budweiser, I read a few chapters in Bruce Chatwin's *In Patagonia*, a great travel book and my current reading project.

The next day I arose early, picked up some bad coffee and a packaged muffin at the convenience store across from the motel, and took off for the trailhead, about thirty miles away. The Talimena Drive is a two-lane highway that curls up and through the mountains from Talihina, Oklahoma to Mena, Arkansas, and presents a beautiful drive. I followed this road on its winding route up to a turnout about a quarter of a mile from the trailhead.

By the time I parked in the turnout and slung on my light backpack, it was daylight with a breeze blowing from the east in my direction. I set off briskly for the trailhead. As I rounded a turn in the road, I saw an animal. It looked like a bear—it *was* a bear, about a two hundred pound brown bear with its head down, smelling for trash along the edge of the highway. The bear was only about a hundred feet away and moving slowly east. I stopped cold and stood stock-still while he lumbered ahead without smelling or seeing me. Suddenly he seemed to hear something and turned and disappeared into the woods. Seeing a bear in Oklahoma isn't exactly like seeing one in Dallas, but it is rare.

After a minute or two to regain my composure, I found the trailhead and started down the trail, or what passed for one. It was rough country—bumpy, hilly, irregular terrain. The trail was marked on the trees with blue paint every few hundred yards or so, but there was really no trail, as such, and hikers had to proceed by aiming at the next marker. If you missed a marker you had to backtrack until you could spot the one that had been missed.

I was soon sweating hard. I had plenty of water, which I drank often, but it was hot and humid in the trees, and after about three hours of slugging along in this rough country, I was getting tired. So after stopping to eat a power bar and an apple, I started back. I never saw the bear again, only a few birds, and was glad to get back to the car after about six hours of hiking.

On the long drive back to Cordell, over two-thirds of the way across the state, I decided the bear was a favorable sign and wrote a poem about him.

THE BEAR FROM OKLAHOMA

The Bear from Oklahoma
Wasn't really out of place
He just wandered west
To find a little space

In Arkansas were other bears
With which he felt real chummy
But the Oklahoma Bear
Couldn't find his favorite honey

He bearly crossed the border
In a place the woods were thick
When he ran across a lawyer
Who was hiking in the sticks

The bear was big and hairy
Built like a big box car
And the lawyer started thinking
He had hiked a little far

The bear did not speak Latin
And couldn't read a writ
And the lawyer quickly figured
That he needed all his wit

So he told the bear a Clinton joke
And made it sound real funny
He got the bear to laughing
And he forgot about his honey

The problem with the lawyer
Was he smelled just like a snack
And the food that he was carrying
Was stuck in his backpack

Things were getting way too tense
But the lawyer caught a break
When the bear happened on to
A nice big juicy snake

The bear was mighty hungry
And that snake tasted plenty fine
And while the bear was eating
The lawyer found a tree to climb

So there's a moral to this story
And a message to this tale
When you go hiking in bear country
Take a pal in your lunch pail

As it turned out, the bear did prove to be a good omen, in a most unexpected way.

CHAPTER 48

I was seeing Dawn regularly. We began making plans and doing things together. I found out she liked to hike, or pretended to, and I took her over to Roman Nose Park for the day. The park is named after Chief Roman Nose, a Cheyenne chief who wintered there with his tribe. The trails are not too long, but wind around in a confusing way, making for short but interesting hiking. I teased Dawn about her Indian heritage, and she teased me about my so-called football prowess.

Life is having something to look forward to, and Dawn became that something in my life. As for her, I provided fun, attention, and entertainment, something she hadn't had much of since her husband left. Maybe the best thing about Dawn was that I finally stopped thinking about Julie, at least most of the time. Long ago I had put Kit out of my mind, but Julie was different. Life was so alive when I was with her that she kept cropping up in my mind long after she was gone. Now Dawn was replacing her, and finally I could move on with my life. Looking back can be constructive to try to avoid making the same mistake twice, but there's no percentage on dwelling in the past. You can't do a damn thing about it anyway, and it always pissed me off when I caught myself worrying about what might have been, instead of what was possible. Dawn was something that was possible—a real, in-the-flesh woman—part of the here and now, and maybe, with a little luck, the future.

Being with her was a release from the day to dayness of my job and the continued efforts to help Don Ed find his witness. I didn't know that it wouldn't be long before events would change my life without any design.

CHAPTER 49

I was about to leave work and head home for my evening run when Mike called me at the sheriff's office.

"Snake, it's time to party. I picked up Butterfly in Oklahoma City; we're goin' over to her daddy's ranch near Elk City to spend the weekend. He's got a pool, a bar, and even his own par three golf course. Come on over."

"Yeah, right. You, me, Butterfly, and Duane Lucas. I thought she couldn't stand her old man."

"She can't. Lucas is gone to New York on business. Butterfly has the key to his spread. We'll be the only ones up there unless you can pick up a cowgirl along the way."

"What about drugs? No illegal drugs. You tend to forget I'm the law."

"I wouldn't do that to you. I told you Butterfly is clean, and I don't smoke dope when she's around. I promise all we'll do is drink Lucas' best whiskey."

"Seeing as the Bushs had other plans this weekend, I guess I'll drop by after I get in my run. How the hell do I get there?"

Mike gave me instructions on how to reach the ranch, and I took of for my evening run. After I finished, cooled down, stretched, and showered, I put on a pair of shorts, a golf shirt, some running shoes, and a baseball hat. I got my seldom-used bathing suit out of the drawer and headed out to meet Mike and the ethereal Butterfly. I had mixed emotions about going to Lucas' ranch. Curiosity, of course, but on the other hand, anything that had to do with Duane Lucas was always unsettling. Just thinking about him made me mad.

As usual, curiosity won out over all of my other emotions. Curiosity has ruled my life and caused me plenty of trouble, but I wouldn't trade it for a safer trait. It's what makes me try things, both those I should, and those I shouldn't. If you're curious, you have to find out what things are like. It's the curious people who take chances intellectually and personally. The other side of the coin is that if you try something, you have to take the consequences. I'd learned that the hard way.

After a few turns off of the interstate, a good two-lane, black top road, led me to Lucas' ranch. No doubt the road was paid for at taxpayers' expense after a well-placed bribe to the right county commissioner. He had a huge, wrought iron gate with "Lucas Ranch" crafted into the frame above the entrance road. His brand was also on the gate, a DL. I thought it should have been $$$.

The gate was open, and I bumped across the cattle guard and drove toward the ranch house on a perfectly maintained road. On one side a herd of prize Black Angus cattle grazed in an open field. A covey of quail burst up on the other side of the road nearer the ranch house.

The house was set by itself several hundred yards away from the barns and other ranch buildings, which were screened by a grove of trees. The road formed a circular drive in front of the house—a huge, rambling, one-story, California-style bungalow. The lawn and flowerbeds were impeccably manicured. I could see a tennis court and one of the greens on Lucas' private golf course behind the house. Mike's battered truck was parked in the driveway.

No one answered the doorbell, so after a couple of minutes, I walked around the side of the house. As I turned the corner of the house, I heard music. It was one of those instruments I never can quite identify, maybe a zither. As I came into the backyard I was able to see a swimming pool. It must have been at least twenty-five meters long, made from pink and gray tile. The pool deck was also tile and obviously expensive. Mike was in the shallow end of the pool, amusing himself by playing with a volleyball. Butterfly lay on a lounging chair, dressed in a skimpy, yellow bikini. The music, which seemed to grow increasingly discordant, was coming from an extensive stereo system with speakers located around the pool area.

"Welcome to Casa Lucas," Mike proclaimed.

"Indeed, welcome to our sanctuary. Please ignore the negative vibes left behind by my father and enjoy the air, space, water, and sounds of this place," Butterfly added.

"What she means is, come on in, the water's fine," Mike advised.

Mike directed me to a cabana located at one end of the pool. The cabana was outfitted with showers, saunas, lockers, and expensively finished with marble floors and ornate hardware. I changed into my bathing suit and returned to the pool area, where I was relieved to hear the Eagles on the stereo. Apparently in my absence, Mike's taste had won out over Butterfly's. It was still hot, and I dove into the swimming pool and then climbed out of the pool and sat down in a chair next to Butterfly.

"In spite of the negative vibrations and cosmic interference of my father's karma, this is still a special place. We have many wonderful birds and animals that live on this ranch. There is even a vortex where only those who are in touch with peace are able to feel its power. I am sure that you will be welcome there, Snake."

"Thanks for the compliment…I think," I responded.

"Butterfly, show him your new tattoo," Mike said.

"Yes, I have a tattoo. It is part of my being and my new beginning." With that, Butterfly pulled down the top of her bikini, showing a small, multi-colored butterfly tattooed on the top of her right breast just above her nipple.

"Now I am truly a butterfly." She said. "And I can fly with Mike. Someday maybe Mike will get a butterfly tattoo."

"Well, it will more likely be a helicopter tattoo," I interjected. "Or maybe a Saber Jet."

"Thanks for your help and support, old buddy," Mike responded.

We lay for sometime in the sun, Mike and I drinking beer and Butterfly entertaining us with occasional indecipherable comments about the state of the universe and the relative merits of various herbs.

Just before it got dark, Butterfly rolled into a sitting position and put her feet down. "I think I'll take a swim," she said. She rose and walked away from us, diving gracefully into the deep end of the pool.

The butterfly on her breast may have been new, but the tattoo on her butt had been there a long time. Just beneath the line of her bikini was an unmistakable small angel playing a harp. I had just become a master detective.

After Butterfly swam for a few minutes, we all decided to change our clothes and fix dinner. I knew I would have to speak with Butterfly but was not sure how to approach the subject. I waited until Mike had gone inside to commandeer two of Lucas' prime steaks for himself and me and a large helping of tofu for Butterfly.

"Butterfly, there's something I need to talk to you about. It's a very serious matter and may involve the life of an innocent man wrongfully charged with a crime."

"I feel his pain," Butterfly responded.

"That's very good, and I'm glad you do. I have to do my job and talk with you about a case. We won't do it tonight, but we have to discuss the possibility that you can help this defendant.

"Snake, I believe that you are a genuine person possessed of positive, humanistic qualities, and I will talk to you about this matter, although I have no idea to what you are referring."

Mike then interrupted our conversation by returning to throw two huge T-bone steaks onto the grill. We ate dinner and I stayed for a while until I began to get drowsy and decided to head for home before I was too sleepy to drive. Butterfly gave me her telephone number in Oklahoma City and I promised to call and set up a meeting in a few days. She said she'd be glad to see me and was not at all inquisitive about my purpose.

CHAPTER 50

Butterfly and I met at the Red Cup, a funky looking coffee shop housed in a converted house near downtown Oklahoma City. The place served good coffee and muffins, and in spite of a less than ideal location off of a major street, always did a brisk business. I got there first and studied the posters on the walls that advertised yoga, offbeat art shows, and musical concerts by unknown bands with odd names. Butterfly came in dressed in a long skirt and a tank top. She didn't have on a bra and her tank top revealed her namesake tattoo. She ordered an herb tea, which she sipped, while I finished my double latté and the remains of a blueberry muffin.

"It's good to see you, Snake, even though you come on a mission which involves great reluctance on your part. You are a friend of my friend, and therefore, you are my friend."

I began to recite Crankcase's story to Butterfly. When I reached the part about Angel approaching Crankcase to buy drugs, she interrupted my story.

"The Angel of Death. The Angel of Death is dead. I know not where she has gone."

"Butterfly, I understand that talking about, or even thinking about, your past life on drugs is painful. I hate to be the one to remind you about things you'd rather forget, but I have to do my job. Even Crankcase doesn't deserve to be wrongfully convicted, and perhaps even executed. I am sure you would agree with me on that point."

"What I am telling you, Snake, is the Angel of Death is dead. I have no memory of the Angel of Death. I cannot help you because I know nothing."

"Butterfly, are you speaking symbolically, or are you telling me that you don't remember anything about Crankcase, or buying drugs from Crankcase, or the night of the murder?"

"Let's go to the park. There is a nice park down the street where we can see birds and sometimes butterflies."

With that Butterfly got up from the table and walked out of the door of the coffee shop, with me close behind. We took my car and drove down the street to a small, but nicely maintained, park. When I stopped the car in the parking lot, Butterfly got out and summoned me to follow. We walked to a picnic table and sat down. It was a pleasant, sunny day with a light breeze blowing. The grass was green and the trees were in bloom. Two young boys were playing an uncoordinated game of tennis on a nearby court. Further across the park it looked like a drug deal was in progress. Pretty much a typical slice of urban life.

"This is a better place. This is a place where butterflies are happy. Now, ask me your questions again."

"Butterfly, if you remember anything at all about meeting or dealing with Crankcase or about the night of the murder, it might help save his life. I'm asking you to help another human being."

For just an instant, Butterfly's eyes hardened and her mouth clinched into a straight line. At that moment I could see for the first time that she was Duane Lucas' daughter and why she had looked familiar when I first met her. "Crankcase and his kind are not human beings. They violated my soul and the soul's of others. They can all rot in hell, where they belong."

"Butterfly, I understand how you feel, but I have to ask you again if there is anything you know that might help Crankcase."

"Angel is dead. I know nothing. Now, Snake, let's go for a walk and enjoy this beautiful day." Arising from the bench, Butterfly took my hand and pulled me along as she began to walk along the path that circled the park. I followed and we strolled at a leisurely pace around the park. As we walked, she gradually relaxed and became her usual spacey self. After we circled the park a few times, as she named all of the flowers and trees and talked to me in her strange, abstract way, she looked at me and said, "Truly, Snake, one night on crack is like every other night on crack. I can't help you. Please don't ask me again."

"I can't promise you that, Butterfly. A man's life is at stake. I'm afraid that's more important than your bad memories, but since you have no recollection of facts, I may not have to bother you again."

She smiled at me benignly as you would at a child.

"I will trust in your kind heart. Now, give me a ride back to my car."

After I dropped Butterfly off and headed west down I-40 toward Cordell, I tried to assess Crankcase's chances. I knew this was a job far better accomplished by Don Ed, who, no doubt, had already considered all of the possibilities, including a witness that wouldn't, or couldn't, cooperate. Like a great chess player, he was probably many moves ahead in the game. All I could do was give him the facts I had found, and he would know how best to use the evidence.

CHAPTER 51

It didn't take me long to find out what Don Ed was thinking. I was bounding up the steps of the courthouse, headed for his chambers, when he came walking out the front door of the courthouse.

"Hold on there, Judge. I've got some important news for you."

"I'm glad to hear that, Sherlock. Let's go over to the café and sit down were we can talk."

We walked across the street to the café and sat down in a booth near the front. The hot sun coming through the window made the booth warm, even though the place was air-conditioned. It was before the dinner hour and after the afternoon coffee break. We were the only ones in the place, except for the waitress and the proprietor. Don Ed ordered coffee, and after the waitress brought it, I told him about finding Angel and how she wouldn't, or couldn't, offer any useful testimony on behalf of Crankcase.

"Judge, can't we just subpoena her? Maybe we could have her pull up her dress and show her tattoo to the jury. What do you think about that?"

Don Ed got a big smile on his face and responded, "Snake, you turned out to be a damned good private investigator. Fortunately, you're not the lawyer who's handling this case. Besides, you don't have all the facts yet. I talked to the public defender in Oklahoma City. He got the lab tests back, and sure enough, there were two blood types on the deceased's clothing. The second blood type is different from Crankcase's. We don't even need a DNA test to prove that someone else's blood was on the deceased's clothes. I'm happy to know that Angel exists and that Crankcase may have been telling the truth about his alibi, but this still may be a case that shouldn't be tried to a jury. I've discussed it with the public defender. He's going to talk to the DA and see what kind of a deal he can make for Crankcase."

"Deal? Hell, Judge, our man is innocent."

"Maybe, but he's still a drug dealer and a thief. Don't forget his fingerprints were all over the taxicab and he had the driver's credit card. His alibi witness is a drug addict who refuses to cooperate, and he's still not credible. Throw in the fact that he's black, and that the DA will probably be able to get a jury of solid, white citizens who hate drugs and crime, and you've still got a tough case to defend. I think there's reasonable doubt. You think there's reasonable doubt. Even a jury might think there's reasonable doubt. But on the other hand, what's to say that Crankcase wasn't there along with someone else and that the two of them killed the taxi driver, or that the blood was already on the taxi driver's shirt?"

"Look, Don Ed, I'm not a lawyer, but I've got a gut feeling that Crankcase didn't do this crime. If you were defending him, I bet you could get a not guilty verdict."

"I appreciate your confidence, Snake, but I've tried too many of these cases to be certain about anything. Before we risk Crankcase's life before a jury, we need to see what the DA will do on a plea bargain. The evidence we've got is enough to force him to make some kind of a deal. I'm almost sure that he'll drop his request for the death penalty and we may be able to do even better. It's horse trading time, and best of all, for the first time, we've got some chips to trade with, due to the lab test and your great sleuthing ability. Tell me some more about this Butterfly character. She interests me, particularly the fact that she's Lucas' daughter. Gratify an old man's morbid curiosity and excite my prurient interest."

"I thought I just heard an old rodeo cowboy talking, instead of some uptight lawyer in a black robe. If it weren't for your bad ticker, sounds to me like you'd be ready to saddle up and ride, or go honky tonkin'. Maybe I should get you in touch with Red. He's the one that seems to know all the spots around this part of the country."

"As young as you are, Snake, even you couldn't keep up with Red. I'm not sure even Mike could."

Our conversation then digressed into the aimless gossip of two old friends. The judge told me he would let me know if the public defender could work out anything with the district attorney.

CHAPTER 52

There was an all-points bulletin out for the arrest of Leland, but nothing happened for several weeks. Morford left the farm quietly and moved in with a cousin, so Lucas got his way, as usual. The highway patrolman recovered enough to go home and then return to limited duty. Spring, with its wild and unpredictable weather, turned to summer, and the farmers prepared for harvest. Then we got a break.

A sheriff in southwest Colorado called. Someone had seen a man that fit Leland's description in a gas station near Ouray. There was also a rumor that some strangers had moved in with "Slidin' Clyde" Gates, a reclusive, local character known to be a gun freak and poacher. Gates lived in an isolated cabin tucked into the side of an almost inaccessible peak in the San Juan Mountains, one of the roughest and wildest areas left in the United States. From the descriptions given to the sheriff, it sounded like the strangers might be Leland and Sherman.

Sheriff Checker was excited and wanted to get to Colorado immediately to take part in any arrest. He called me into his office and said, "Snake, we need to get our butts out to Colorado, ASAP. I want to catch these bastards myself after all the grief they caused around here. Let's start right away and take turns driving. We'll be there in about twelve or fourteen hours, I figure."

"I got a better idea, Sheriff. I'll get Mike to fly us out. Surely the county can pay for the gas."

"You want me to fly with that crazy son of a bitch? This job doesn't call for combat pay!"

"Mike's really a hell of a pilot. He just likes to scare himself. He's got a Baron that can really move. We'll be out there in less than three hours."

"If I say yes, you'll know how bad I want these guys. So I'm sayin' yes. Call Mike and set it up. I'll tell the Colorado sheriff we're on our way."

Mike was excited and said he'd pick us up at the Cordell airport. He wanted to know if the sheriff would make him a deputy and issue him a sidearm. When I said no, he was disappointed but still up for the trip. Any kind of excitement always turned him on.

When we got to the airport, Mike had landed his plane. He had on an old army fatigue shirt from his Vietnam days, blue jeans, and cowboy boots. He couldn't find the fatigue pants and helmet that he wore in the service, but was reporting for action. He said he wanted to be a deputy since, as he put it, he was part of the posse. The sheriff had to turn him down again, but he was somewhat pacified when he was promised his charter rate for flying us to Colorado.

The sheriff and I each brought shotguns, armored vests, and plenty of ammunition. If there was trouble, we wanted to be ready.

CHAPTER 53

We loaded up and took off from the Cordell airport into what looked like dark rain clouds. The sheriff was a white-knuckle flyer, and he clung to the arms of his seat with a death grip as his face turned a pale shade of gray. The fact that he was in the plane at all showed how much he wanted to catch Leland and Sherman.

Mike took the baron up in a steady climb to 15,000 feet and headed west at about 240 knots. We flew out over western Oklahoma and the Texas panhandle and then crossed over into the mountains of northern New Mexico and southern Colorado. We could see snow high on the peaks of the San Juans as Mike brought the plane down for a perfect landing in Montrose.

The local sheriff met us at the airport. He looked like the man in the Marlboro ad. Tall and slim with a weathered-looking face, he was dressed in cowboy hat, blue jeans, boots, a vest, and sported a big belt buckle. No doubt he was elected sheriff because he looked the part. He introduced himself as Sheriff Jackson, but the man behind the desk at the airport called him "Slim." So now we had Chubby and Slim chasing the bad guys.

Sheriff Jackson gave Mike a funny look, but relaxed a little when the sheriff identified Mike as the pilot. We piled into the sheriff's big SUV and headed for Ouray. We began to climb up into the San Juans and wound our way into Ouray, a town of about seven hundred people, completely surrounded by towering peaks rising on all sides.

This is some of the most rugged country in the United Sates, with jagged mountains rising above 14,000 feet. The Rockies in this part of Colorado are covered with thick pine and aspen forests at lower elevations, and with barren rock and scree fields above the timberline. Scree is loose rock and dirt found on steep mountainsides, which has enough friction to stay where it is until you step on it, and then slides downhill. Trying to go uphill in scree is like climbing in mashed potatoes; you slide back three quarters of a step for each step up you take. Coming down on scree is like riding a skateboard with the dirt in front of you moving downhill.

Some of the best hiking, camping, and fishing in the world is in the San Juans, but the terrain is rugged and the weather violent and unpredictable. The winters are harsh, snow stays at higher altitudes year round, and rain, hail, and lightening storms can strike quickly and render the exposed mountain slopes dangerous for lightening strikes and avalanches. Like all wild areas, the power of nature is omnipresent.

As we drove up the valley in crisp, clear weather, Sheriff Jackson told us about Slidin' Clyde Gates. He got his nickname from slidin' out of trouble. Every game ranger in western Colorado knew that Clyde was a poacher, who killed deer, elk, beaver, ducks, and marmots whenever and in whatever quantity he wanted, with total disregard for all game laws. Even though they knew what Clyde did, they couldn't catch him, no matter how hard they tried. Clyde knew the woods and rarely went anywhere except on foot, even in the winter when he navigated the mountains on snow shoes and cross-country skis. He could move through the forests and canyons of this wild country like an Indian and disappear into areas where no trails existed and no landmarks were available. Clyde was heavily armed with rifles and shotguns, but most of his hunting was done with traps and snares. He had a record for game law violations, but hadn't been arrested in years, and for the most part the local rangers had given up trying to catch him.

It was widely believed that Clyde had helped the three survivalists who had killed a policeman near Cortez and then vanished into the southern Colorado wilderness in the summer of 1998. One of the killers quickly committed suicide, and the remains of another were found a year later, but the third had still never been accounted for, even though a massive manhunt had been conducted by state and federal authorities, and even Native American trackers. Rumor was that the fugitives, who were the homeboys of this mountainous neighborhood, had gotten help with food and supplies, and that Clyde furnished the help.

The men who fit the description of Leland and Sherman were driving an Explorer when seen at a gas station near Ouray. Later the same vehicle was seen by some hikers, high up on a four-wheel drive trail in the area of Clyde's cabin. Based on Clyde's history, this sounded like a good lead on Leland and Sherman.

Sheriff Jackson had learned of these sightings by accident when talking to the gas station employee in Ouray, who off-handedly mentioned, "two mean-looking hombres," one of whom had a skull and crossbones tattooed on his shoulder, the other a big, menacing man dressed in military fatigues.

The first question that had to be answered was how to carry out the arrest of Leland and Sherman. As described by Sheriff Jackson, getting to Clyde's cabin and making an arrest would be a dangerous matter. The cabin was located on a remote mountain slope at about 10,000 feet. It was over a mile to the cabin from the end of a rough and rocky jeep road that ended at an abandoned mine. From the mine, a steep trail wound up the side of the mountain, the last quarter mile across an open meadow, which would expose anyone approaching the cabin to the clear view of its occupants and provide an open field of fire from the cabin. Dense woods closed in from behind the cabin, stretching up the mountain to the tree line, where scree led to sheer rocky cliffs that rose to a crest at over 12,000 feet.

The game rangers believed that the whole meadow was booby-trapped and mined with homemade land mines. Approaching the cabin from the trailhead at the mine would be dangerous if not suicidal. Furthermore, if the cabin's occupants detected any unwanted visitors, they could disappear into the woods on a moment's notice. Clyde had created a stronghold.

The two sheriffs decided to wait until near dark and proceed up the mine road to its terminus, to see if they could locate Leland's vehicle and confirm his presence at the cabin without being discovered. We stopped in Ouray to get gas, drink coffee, and talk strategy. Mike was quickly bored, and he and I decided to walk around town. Mike bought some cheap ornate candles for Butterfly, and I picked up a few postcards with dramatic photographs of mountain peaks and brilliant foliage. It began to get dark, and the four of us got back in the sheriff's car and headed out to reconnoiter. We turned off a paved road onto a bumpy, dirt and gravel road, and then after about three miles, onto a four-wheel drive track that led to a tooth-jarring, axle-bursting ride over washed out gullies and ridges. Dusk began to turn to darkness as we bounced our way uphill.

Finally, the sheriff pulled over and gave us flashlights and we began to climb on foot. After about five minutes, Sheriff Checker needed to stop and rest, gasping for breath and complaining about the altitude. I could tell it was even bothering Mike, and although I wouldn't admit it, I could also feel the effects. After a brief rest, we forged on for another few minutes until we could see the outline of the structures that made up the abandoned mine property. Sheriff Jackson told us to shut off our flashlights and follow him as he moved in an easy, sure-footed stride up the dark slope toward the mine. We strung out behind, huffing and puffing, until we reached a relatively flat spot and came upon an Explorer pulled into the edge of the woods. The sheriff switched on his light long enough to see the license plate. It was a New Mexico plate, splattered with mud, but legible. In spite of the change of plates, we were sure this was Leland's vehicle. The sheriff wrote down the plate number and pointed to a faint break in what otherwise appeared to be impenetrable forest, which he identified as the beginning of the trail to Clyde's cabin, which according to him, was far steeper than the road we had just ascended.

We clumsily clamored down to the sheriff's vehicle with a minimum amount of slipping and falling. On the drive back to Ouray, we talked about the difficulty of getting to Clyde's cabin, and the merits of trying to wait on Leland or Sherman to come down where they would be more vulnerable to arrest. In the meantime, Sheriff Jackson got on his radio to get a warrant and to set-up surveillance at the bottom of the jeep road to pick up the Explorer if it came down from the mine to the highway. He also had his office run the New Mexico plates, which turned out to be stolen.

We were gathered around a table at a bar in Ouray, when Sheriff Checker said, "Slim, is there any other way into that cabin, or is that a stupid question?"

"I'm not sure, but I know how to find out. There's a local boy here in town that has roamed these mountains all of his life. He's an ultra marathon runner, hiker, and rock climber. If there's another way in there he'd know it. I'm going to get hold of him and see what he says."

Sheriff Jackson then called Ron Alvarez, and asked him to join us. While we waited for Ron, the sheriff told us more about him.

"Have you ever heard of a hundred mile race called the 'Hardrock?'"

None of us had, so the sheriff went on to fill us in on the race and Ron's background. As Sheriff Jackson described it to us, the Hardrock was more a test of survival than a race. The course wound through the San Juans in a hundred-mile loop, beginning and ending at Silverton. The participants had to climb to over 12,000 feet eleven times. They ran through snow and ice, rocks and scree, and some of them carried ice axes to help navigate various stretches of the race. The contestants were required to finish in forty-eight hours, although Ron had run the race in around thirty hours, winning three times. He had also won the Pike's Peak marathon and was widely acknowledged as one of the greatest high-altitude trail runners of all time.

Ron had grown up around Ouray and as a young man, hiked, camped, and climbed all over the surrounding mountains. He made his living as a surveyor for the state of Colorado, but his real passion was distance running. A tall, slim, Hispanic-looking man, with deep, black eyes and black hair, he stood over six feet in height and could not have weighed over 160 pounds, but rather than looking thin, he appeared more lanky and tough. Oddly built with extremely long legs, Ron looked like some kind of high mountain animal, which he was.

Ron sat down, and after introducing everyone, the sheriff asked him, "Is there any way into Clyde's cabin, other than up the trail from the old mine?"

"Let's get a topo map and we'll see," Ron responded.

Ron went to his car and returned to the table with a USGS topographic map of the area around Clyde's cabin. After pinpointing the cabin, Ron and Sheriff Jackson began to discuss possible routes from other trails or roads. After some discussion, the sheriff was ready to conclude that no alternative to the trail across the meadow existed. Ron, however, kept studying the map and finally announced, "I think it can be done." He then began to trace an irregular line on the map with a pencil. Ron suggested that a strong climber could bushwhack his way about sixteen miles up the western slope of the mountain behind where Clyde's cabin perched, and then descend by way of a series of climbs and rappels some two miles to the timberline above the cabin, and thence through the woods to the cabin itself.

"You mean you think you could do it?" the sheriff said. "Hell, you can do things real people wouldn't even consider. I need to know if I can get some armed law enforcement officers into position to take these guys by surprise. Can they do it?"

"Depends," Ron replied.

"Depends on what?"

"Who they are."

The sheriff looked around the table and then pointed at me. "How about Snake?"

Ron paused a second and then said, "Maybe, if he's fit."

"How about Grindle?"

Ron got a big smile on his face at the mention of Grindle. "I'd go up there with Grindle just to see him try. He'd die before he'd admit he couldn't do it, and that's just what might happen."

The sheriff laughed and then told us about Grindle. He was an ex–high school jock from Durango, and a big hunter and fisherman. Sort of a poster boy for the NRA, he fancied himself a stud who was stronger and tougher than anyone. He was one of the sheriff's deputies and clearly had his eye on Sheriff Jackson's job. It worried me immediately when I found out he hadn't been given a nickname by the other deputies.

The sheriff then asked Ron for a more detailed description of the route he proposed. As Ron described it, the first eight miles or so was a little-used hunting trail, steep but fairly decent walking conditions. After that, it would take a climb through a pine and then aspen forest for another six miles, and then an ascent of over 2,000 feet across scree and boulders over the last two to three miles to the summit. As if that wasn't hard enough, there would still be snow and ice near the top of the climb. Coming down would be faster, but a lot more dangerous—a rappel and then a "glissade," a fancy term for sliding on your ass. The climbers would have to carry water, food for energy, and of course, plenty of firepower. Ron made it clear he was quite willing to attempt the climb, but had no intention of taking part in any assault on Clyde's cabin.

"That Clyde is one crazy, mean dude," as Ron put it. "He hates everybody, but mostly the government. If you go on to his property, you better be ready to bring him out feet first."

When questioned further by Sheriff Jackson, Ron estimated the whole operation would take at least twelve to fourteen hours. This brought on another problem—timing. Climbing in the dark would be difficult, although we could start on the trail using head lamps or flashlights, and approaching the cabin in daylight, even from a surprising direction, could be even more dangerous. A night on the mountain would require tents and sleeping bags and was something even Ron did not recommend. These options led to another round of discussion.

Finally, Sheriff Jackson and Chubby came up with a plan. Ron would lead the climb, accompanied by Grindle and me. Grindle and I would carry weapons and armored vests. Otherwise, we would all pack as little as possible. We would start just before daylight and seek to reach the top within twelve hours or less. We would then try to time our descent so we could sneak in through the woods behind the cabin to be ready for an assault by dusk of the same day. The most dangerous part of the whole operation would be trying to get close to the cabin without alerting the suspects. Assuming we pulled this off, Grindle and I would go in fully armed to make the arrest, while the sheriff and his other deputies stood ready to back us up from the bottom of the meadow facing the cabin. It may not have been a great plan, but it was the only one we could come up with, so it would have to do.

The sheriff called Grindle and told him to meet us at the local sporting goods store. The proprietor was summoned to open the store so we could assemble the proper gear for the climb. Luckily, I had worn my well-used hiking boots, anticipating a need to travel by foot in the mountains.

Grindle showed up, and as advertised, immediately tried to take charge of the operation. He was a big man, about six foot four and two hundred and twenty pounds, solidly built, and handsome in a cruel, kind of Elvis Presley, way. It was clear that he and Ron did not get along—Ron in a quiet but pointed way, and Grindle in a more obvious fashion. As soon as he heard the plan, Grindle began to criticize the route and question the need to have Ron involved. Then he tried to bully Ron into changing the timing. After a few blustering tirades, the sheriff had to step in and take control.

"Shut up, Grindle. These are my orders and you'll follow them, or I'll get someone else to make the climb."

Grindle quieted down and, although his eyes still reflected his defiance, deferred to the sheriff. There was no way he would miss this chance to be a hero and capture the fugitives at the cabin.

The sheriff continued. "Ron's in charge until you get to the tree line above the cabin. He leads the climb, and I don't want any shit from you, Grindle. Once you are in the trees above the cabin, you're in charge, Grindle. You and Snake need to set up to make the arrest. That's the way it is, whether you like it or not!"

After the sheriff's proclamation, Grindle backed off from Ron, but still had to show his knowledge of the mountains and the gear we needed by frequent reference to his hunting experiences, with elaborate accounts of his physical prowess.

In spite of Grindle, Ron went about his business in a calm, methodical way. He had each of us lay out exactly what we would carry and then furnished us the equipment he knew we would require.

Grindle and I each had our Glocks, holsters, and cartridge belts. Grindle insisted on taking a 12-gauge shotgun and a box of double ought slugs. The shotgun had a carrying sling, but Ron still didn't like the idea of the gun. The sheriff sided with Grindle, knowing the men in the cabin would be heavily armed. Both Grindle and I also had to wear armored vests. I also packed what looked like a flare gun that fired teargas canisters, along with two canisters.

Ron then selected backpacks, ice axes, and crampons that fit onto our boots. Each of us then picked out a good rain suit, in case the fickle mountain weather changed during the day. Ron put together what he called a climbing rig, which included ropes, pitons, and a piece of equipment known as a Jumaran Ascender.

After we carefully packed our gear and filled our packs until they were as comfortable as possible, we talked about water and food. We would each carry a camelback that held a hundred ounces of water. I knew from experience I would also need some Gatorade to avoid dehydration and possible altitude sickness. Ron would also carry some iodine pills and a canteen in case we had to try to use snow or stream water for drinking. As to food, Ron just said, "Suit yourself, but make it light. The less you carry, the better you'll feel."

By the time we finished our outfitting, it was about eleven o'clock. We would have to leave at about 3:00 a.m. to reach our trailhead before daylight. Although it was only about twenty miles away as the crow flies, we weren't crows, which meant we had about a forty-mile drive around the mountains to the trailhead on the Western slope of the mountain, toward Telluride.

CHAPTER 54

After a few hours of sleep at a motel, where the sheriff had arranged for rooms, I was awakened at 3:00 a.m. by a knock on the door. I dressed hurriedly in sturdy khaki pants, a T-shirt, and a long-sleeve, lightweight shirt and a rain jacket. Ron and Grindle were waiting for me in Grindle's SUV. I threw my pack into the back and we took off for the trailhead.

We stopped at Ridgway and bought Gatorade, power bars, dried fruit, cookies, and bagels. I drank watery coffee from a Styrofoam cup and listened to Grindle tell lies about his great hunting adventures. Just before we got to the turn for Telluride, Ron directed Grindle up an old jeep road. In a few minutes, Ron consulted his topo map, and then twenty minutes later told Grindle to slow down and creep along. Within less than a quarter mile, Ron called for a stop. I could see nothing from the car, but after we got out, Ron pointed to what was a faint trail leading into the darkness of the adjacent woods.

It was still dark as we shouldered our packs and headed up the trail with Ron in the lead, Grindle next, and me at the rear. We used headlamps to follow the faint track of the trail through the thick pine forest. Somewhere in front of us a small animal moved, rustling the bushes along the trail, and we could hear birds taking wing and chirping in the trees.

We moved at a steady pace up the trail for over two hours. The terrain began to steepen, and dark began to turn to dawn. The walking was fairly good, although certainly not the type of maintained trail I was familiar with from my recreational hiking. The unaccustomed pack felt heavy, even though it only weighed about twenty pounds.

The armored vest was already uncomfortable, but I knew there was no choice as to this protection.

We waded through a small stream, and then Ron slowed his pace. He stopped and, removing his GPS, consulted his topo map again.

"Ok, boys, this is about as good a place as any to start our climb. We need to stay together. We'll stop every hour or so, but if you need water or rest, we'll all stop together. Follow me."

With no further direction, Ron turned and led us into the forest. It was still dark in the woods. The sun was up, but blocked by the mountains, and only a few small shafts of light were filtering through the dense canopy of trees. The ground began to slope up more steeply, but walking was not too hard, mostly on a bed of pine needles interspersed with some tangled bushes. We kept up a steady pace for over an hour until we came to the edge of a deep, rock-strewn ravine. The sides of the ravine were steep and covered with boulders, trees, and brush. Ron stopped and again consulted his topo map. After a few minutes of study, he set out along the edge of the ravine, perpendicular to our intended route. This immediately provoked comment from Grindle.

"What the hell, Ron! We can get down and out of that ditch right here. Besides, you always walk downstream, never upstream. You're fucking us up already."

Before Ron could answer, I spoke up. "Shut up, Grindle. You know the sheriff put Ron in charge of the climb."

"So, the flatlander speaks. Don't be a brownnose for the sheriff. I know these mountains like the back of my hand. This ravine just gets worse in this direction," Grindle said, but he did follow, now bringing up the rear.

Unfortunately for a while it looked like Grindle was right. The ravine got steeper, deeper, and rockier. Finally, after about thirty minutes of walking, the ravine narrowed and became less deep.

Crossing the ravine would still be difficult. We would have to clamber down steep and slippery boulders through heavy brush and then climb up a similar slope on the other side. Ron didn't think we needed to be roped, and after checking our packs we began to climb down into the ravine. Ron was nimble and light and had little trouble. Grindle and I, on the other hand, were forced to descend slowly and awkwardly as we searched for footholds and handholds and, in some cases, partially slid and partially fell down the side of slippery rocks. We had to concentrate to avoid falling, as twisting an ankle, or worse yet breaking something, would end our mission. The bushes and weeds scratched our faces and hands as the sun began to break through the clouds. My shirt was soaked with sweat when I finally slid, backward and feet first, to a clumsy landing at the bottom of the ravine. Grindle, red faced and sweating, followed close behind.

We took off our packs and rested for a few minutes while we drank water, and then set off up the opposite slope for the climb to the top, some five hundred feet above. Once again, Ron moved in a sure-footed, methodical way up and over the boulders and around the brush. Grindle and I labored upward at a much slower pace, with frequent false starts, backtracks, and long pauses to get back our wind. My legs were already aching, and I didn't relish the prospect of more hours of climbing. At the top we again rested. Ron perused his map and referred to his GPS. He appeared to be as fresh as when we had started and was barely sweating.

It was about eleven o'clock as we resumed our upward climb through the continuing pine forest. Occasionally, Ron would start to pull away from us and have to slow down so we weren't left behind. Sometime in the next hour, the trees changed to aspens and then began to thin as we crossed a number of high mountain meadows. The meadows were still wet from the melting snow above and made for slow, muddy progress.

About two in the afternoon we reached the tree line and came on to an open area of what looked like tundra stretching up to the edge of a scree field that was partly covered by snow. The footing was much better, but the slope was the steepest we had encountered. We were now climbing, not walking, proceeding upward one laborious step at a time. Working hard, we reached the beginning of the scree by 3:00 p.m. I had drunk three liters of water and almost all of my Gatorade. The good news was my pack was lighter, but the bad news was I wasn't sure I had enough remaining to finish the climb. I asked Ron if he thought we should try to melt some snow, but he preferred to keep going until we reached the top.

We began to climb the scree field, which proved as treacherous and slippery as predicted. Grindle and I were sliding back with almost every step, climbing almost on all fours, but we kept moving upward until we reached the bottom edge of the snow. It was more ice than snow, melting and wet, at first slushy and then a harder surface. At this point, Ron told us to unsling our ice axes and attach the crampons to our boots. We roped ourselves together, and we began the ascent of the snowfield. In order to reach the point above on the rock cliff where we could climb up and over the mountain, we had to climb at an angle veering south to our right across the slick and glassy surface. It was like walking sideways up an inverted ice rink. Each step required setting your foot down flat to build a weight-supporting surface for the next step. Needless to say, our progress was slow.

Suddenly, Grindle slipped, fell, and began sliding backward down the ice. Before I knew what had happened, the rope jerked me off of my feet and down the slope on my ass. Ron quickly jammed his ice axe into the ice, braced himself, and stopped our slide. Grindle and I both sunk our axes into the ice and Ron managed to keep his balance without falling. Cursing, Grindle climbed back up using his axe and crampons until the rope was slack. Then he and I slowly regained a place on the mountain horizontal with Ron where we could again proceed upward.

The sun was intense and reflected off of the ice. We all wore dark glasses and stopped frequently to rest. Although it could not have been more than a half mile across the ice, it took us fully an hour to reach the upper edge where we flopped down exhausted from the effort, only to look upward at our next challenge.

Our final ascent to the top would take us up a rocky crevasse to the notch in the mountain where we could cross to the other side. Ron gazed up at the route and for the first time showed some concern. While Grindle and I sprawled on the ground trying to recover our legs and wind, Ron moved up toward the bottom of the crevasse in order to get a better look at what was ahead. When he returned he looked at us and said, "That crevasse is not shaped the way that I thought it was. It is going to take some rock climbing to get to the top. We can scramble the first part and then wedge in through that chimney, but the last fifty feet we're going to have to climb. Do either of you have any experience in rock climbing?"

"You son of a bitch, Ron! I told the sheriff you didn't know what you were doing, and that you'd either get us lost or killed up here. I didn't sign on to break my neck rock climbing, I came to arrest criminals," Grindle quickly replied.

"I take it that means you don't have any experience rock climbing," I said. "Neither do I."

"Well, we'll either have to go up or down. I don't look forward to climbing with two climbers who have never climbed before," Ron said. "But I think it can be done."

"If you kill us, you little fucker, I'll make you live to regret it," Grindle said, which enlisted a smile from Ron and guffaw from me.

The situation reminded me of how I learned to ski. When I was as Stanford, a friend of mine who was an experienced skier took me up to Squaw Valley. After a few runs on the bunny slope, we took a lift to the top of an intermediate run. He looked at me and said, "I'll see you at the bottom," as he disappeared down the run. There was no choice but to follow him down, and after a few falls, I began to get the hang of skiing. It looked like I was going to learn rock climbing the same way.

Ron suggested that we all leave our packs and carry only what was necessary. Grindle refused to leave the shotgun, and I was reluctant to part with the tear gas gun and canisters, but I finally took Ron's suggestion, although Grindle kept the shotgun. Ron unslung his climbing rope, checked his other equipment, and gave us a short course on rock climbing. The concept didn't seem too hard with our feet under us on a firm surface. It wouldn't be long before we learned that climbing was something like dancing on air. It takes a great leap of faith and plenty of confidence to be a good climber. Visualize standing on a pointed rock the size of a quarter and letting go with both hands and the other foot to reach up for the next handhold which is about the same size. Do this again and again, and you may reach the top. It's a matter of balance, and more of an art than a science.

Ron knew all this well and had devised a plan to get us to the top. He would climb up himself and secure the rope which he would drop to us. Then Grindle and I would each climb using an ascender attached to the hanging rope, a technique Ron described as top roping.

We drank the last of our water and piled our packs against a rock to be picked up the "next time we come this way," as Ron said.

We climbed to the base of the cliffs to reach what Ron called a chimney. When we reached the chimney, Ron placed his back against one side of the rocks and his feet and hands against the other and began to squirm upward using the two sides of the chimney to support himself. Grindle and I followed in a similar manner until we reached the top of the chimney. At that point, Ron turned and faced the sheer wall of the cliff, reached up, drove a piton into the wall with a hammer, attached the rope and then began to ascend by inserting his feet and his hands into cracks and irregular ledges in the side of the cliff, some so small he was literally hanging by the tips of his fingers and toes. Grindle and I stayed perched at the top of the chimney.

Ron climbed slowly, but steadily, up the almost vertical wall of the cliff, until he reached what appeared to be a ledge, albeit a very narrow one. At that point he stopped and secured himself and then the rope. He then threw the rope down to where we stood at the apex of the chimney. I attached what Ron had called an ascender—a metal, hinged apparatus—to the rope, and then I began to climb.

No doubt this was a rudimentary climb for an experienced climber like Ron, something like King Kong ascending the Empire State building, but to me it was a tense ordeal. The sweat rolled down my face, hands, and arms. My body was already tired and sore from hours of hiking and climbing. Sometimes I had to stop on a precarious purchase and lean against the rope, catch my wind, and regain my strength. It was a grueling and laborious task, heightened by a fear of falling in spite of the rope. As I climbed higher, I refused to look down and tried to concentrate on holding on and trusting Ron. In this manner, I finally inched my way to the ledge, and with great relief, pulled myself up next to Ron. Unfortunately, at this point I had to unhook from the rope and rely on my death grip of the handholds above the ledge and my precarious balance. Grindle then followed me up in the same manner. We all pressed ourselves against a rock wall and inched our way along the ledge to what appeared to be the crest of the mountain. At the top, a slightly wider ledge and notch appeared through the rocks. All three of us were able to gather on this natural platform to look down on the other side.

CHAPTER 55

L ooking down the mountain, what we saw was not encouraging: another sheer rock cliff that plummeted down to a scree field much like the one we had ascended to reach the top.

"We'll have to rappel to the top of the scree field," Ron said.

At least rappelling was something we had talked about and something I had actually done a few times.

"I think we have enough rope for a rappel all the way to the bottom," Ron said.

"'Think' don't mean shit," Grindle replied. "I'm tired of your thinkin'. It damn near got us all killed."

"Grindle, you can either rappel or you can jump, I frankly don't give a shit," I responded.

"And a good day to you too, asshole," Grindle replied.

Ron, with his usual concentration, simply began preparing for the rappel by driving pitons into a flat surface near the downhill side of the ledge. He then attached the rope, threw it over the side, and let it play down. The remaining end of the rope he wrapped around my waist and showed me how to use it to descend.

"If there's not enough rope to get to the bottom, when you reach the end of the rope, brake against the wall, find a place to hang on and climb down. Now, turn around and step off backward."

And that's what I did. There's something about that moment when you step backward high above solid ground that just can't be described. No matter how safe you think it might be, instinctively you know that man wasn't made to fly, and your stomach drops down before the rest of your body can follow. Once in the air, I let myself down slowly until I reached almost the end of the rope. Looking down I could see that I was near the bottom, but there was no way the rope would reach all the way to the top of the scree field. I tried to control my descent and look for a place to get a grip on the rock before I let loose of the rope, but there was not a good handhold available. The only thing to do was let go and drop. And drop I did, probably six or eight feet where I hit, bounced, and slid down the scree field some twenty or thirty feet before I came to rest. I was shaken but unhurt, other than both hands and the side of my face being scratched by the scree.

I recovered enough to watch Grindle make his awkward way down to the end of the rope. He was able to find a place to wedge his foot and then his hand against the side of the wall before he let go of the rope, and thus climb down with less of a problem. Ron then came down, climbed down the wall, and landed easily. We assembled at the top of the scree field and looked down to where the tree line began, a mile or more below. Down the slope in the distance we were just able to see the top of what appeared to be Clyde's cabin.

After viewing the scree field, Ron suggested a glissade rather than an attempt to keep our feet on the way down. He went first and Grindle and I followed, sliding on our asses down the crumbling scree. It was something like going down a big slide, and probably the first time during the whole trip that I hadn't been exhausted or scared.

We all crashed to a halt at the end of the scree field, and after righting ourselves, began a downward climb to the tree line. While the dangerous part of the climb was over in one way, in another, it had just begun. We were descending across rock-strewn, open ground, and if the occupants of the cabin for any reason decided to look up the mountain, they could see us approaching. Even taking into consideration the dangers we had already survived, being detected by Leland, Sherman, and Clyde was the worst hazard yet. Finally we entered the tree line at about 11,000 feet. At this point, Grindle called a halt.

"I'm in charge now. I'll lead. Snake, you follow. Ron, you stay the hell out of the way. We're goin' down to get into position above the cabin. First I'll call the sheriff and make sure he's ready to back us up when we make the arrest, then Snake and I will get into position where I can make the arrest and Snake can back me. When we see how they're set up, we'll decide how best to approach the cabin."

It was now evening and the light was beginning to fade. It was important to get into position before dark, so down we went again through the trees. I could tell by the way he walked that Grindle was as tired as I was, but to his credit, he kept going and never mentioned his fatigue. Even Ron looked a little tired, although he still moved easily compared to Grindle and me.

As it began to get dusky, Grindle stopped us again. He tried to reach the sheriff on his cell phone and advise him that we had made the climb and were getting into position above the cabin, but had no luck. Grindle then ordered Ron to stay put. We checked our weapons and proceeded down through the trees toward the cabin. When we reached a point about one hundred yards from the cabin, we stopped again.

We were approaching the cabin from the rear and could see the roof and the back wall. It was a rough, wooden structure with a green, asphalt tile roof, an outhouse, and a small corral that held two mules. Firewood was stacked against the side of the cabin, and there were no windows facing uphill. The woods came within twenty or thirty yards of the back of the cabin. There was no movement or sign of life outside the cabin itself, except the mules.

Grindle decided we would spread out about twenty yards apart and approach the cabin slowly through the trees until we reached the edge of the open space behind the structures. We would then maneuver around the cabin to determine where the subjects were located. Grindle would go in first, and I would stay in position to provide cover for him. We crept through the woods making as little noise as possible until we reached the tree line.

We were moving forward through the trees when I heard the snarling bark of a big dog and saw Leland come around the corner of the cabin carrying a rifle. Grindle stood up, stepped out of the trees, raised his shotgun, and in his best cop voice proclaimed, "You're under arrest, drop the gun." Leland never paused as he lifted and fired his rifle. Grindle fired back with the shotgun but missed. Leland scrambled back around the corner of the cabin and snapped off another shot, which hit Grindle, knocking him backward off of his feet.

A man armed with a rifle came out from the other side of the cabin, running low across the open area, and then disappearing into the trees uphill from the cabin. I didn't recognize him and figured it was Clyde. I started to circle around the side of the cabin, staying in the trees and trying to get a line of sight on Leland. Before I got far, Leland burst around the cabin, running for the tree line. I snapped off a shot that missed and then turned to try to cut him off from the trees. He angled away from me, running uphill, and gave me a chance for another shot. This time I didn't miss. The bullet hit him and he went down, but got up and staggered toward the tree line still grasping his rifle. He made it into trees, and I had no choice but to try to cut across and intercept his path. Moving from tree to tree without giving Leland a target, I tried to keep up my pace so he wouldn't disappear into the forest. It was getting dark and hard to see in the trees. I didn't think I could find Leland if he just stayed hidden, but he didn't. I heard the shot and sensed the bullet passing through the trees above my head. I hit the ground and then began to crawl to my right, trying to change my position before Leland got off another shot. From the sound of his rifle, I knew his position and wanted to spot him for a clear shot.

As I was about to rise up to risk a look, a huge, brown dog came hurtling out of the grass behind me. I threw my arm up just in time to intercept its closing jaws as it leapt on me. The force and weight of the dog knocked me backward off of my feet with the dog on top. I clung to my pistol with the other hand, and as we rolled in the dirt with the dog biting at my arm and throat, somehow I was able to bring the gun up and shoot the dog in the head at point-blank range. Blood, bone, and brains splattered all over my chest and face as the dog flopped dead onto the ground.

Another shot from Leland passed by, this one way too close. I could almost feel the bullet. Again I moved, rolling so as not to give Leland another target. As I lay on the ground, slightly dazed and covered with the dog's blood and brains, another shot ricocheted off a tree above my head. I rolled into the bushes, and then crouching, began to move to once again try to flank Leland from an uphill position. At that moment, an explosion shook the ground around me and brought leaves fluttering down from the trees. It came from the direction of the cabin. I later learned it was a mine that had been set off intentionally by the sheriff, who was moving up with his men across the meadow. They had borrowed a mine detector from the National Guard unit in Durango and were using it to guide them up the trail across the meadow to the cabin.

The explosion must have startled Leland, too. While my ears were still ringing, I could see him move in the trees some fifty yards away. But before I could get off a shot, I heard the deep boom of a shotgun and Leland fell in a heap, disappearing from view. Grindle yelled out, "Stay down, Snake, there may be somebody else in here." I stayed put for a few minutes until Grindle yelled again, "Come on up here, but stay low and keep an eye out for that other guy that ran into the woods." I moved up and reached Grindle and Leland. Leland lay on the ground, shot twice, but still barely alive. He was hit once high in the shoulder, a superficial looking wound, which was the bullet I had snapped off at him as he ran from the cabin. Grindle had hit him in the back just above his waist. The double ought shot had blown a hole almost all the way through him and he was bleeding profusely. Grindle stood over him still holding his shotgun.

"I thought you were shot, Grindle."

"Well, I guess lugging these armored vests all the way up that mountain wasn't such a bad idea after all. Grindle said as he pointed to where the bullet had lodged in his armored vest.

As much as Grindle irritated me, I had to agree with him this time.

I pulled off my shirt and wadded it into the hole in Leland's back. He was making strange gurgling sounds, and blood, foam, and spittle was drooling from his mouth.

"The guy that ran was Clyde. It's getting dark and there's no use in trying to track him in these woods. He's half way to Utah by now," Grindle said. "Let's get this piece of shit down the mountain and see what the sheriff's found at the cabin."

CHAPTER 56

We each got one of Leland's arms over our shoulders. I took his rifle in one hand, and Grindle and I half carried, half dragged Leland to the edge of the woods and then laid him in the clearing behind the cabin. Sheriff Jackson, Sheriff Checker, and five or six other deputies came around the cabin, heavily armed and wearing armored vests.

"There's nobody in the cabin," Sheriff Jackson said. "That means Clyde and Sherman got away somehow."

I responded, "Here's Leland, or what's left of him."

"You boys don't look so damn good yourselves. I'm not sure who won this fight," Sheriff Jackson said.

"Well, we ain't dead, but it sure isn't that little shit Ron's fault," Grindle responded.

"Where is Ron?"

Before we could answer, Ron came stumbling out of the trees. His gait was unsteady, and he had a dazed look on his face. There was blood running down from one eyebrow and the bruise around his eye was going to make a huge shiner. He had a piece of cloth clutched in his hand and his legs were wobbly as he walked slowly toward us. "He got away," Ron said. "I saw Clyde running in the trees. I know you told me not to get involved in the arrest, but I couldn't stand it. I ran him down and tackled him. He packs a hell of a punch. I tore a piece of his shirt grabbing him, but he knocked the crap out of me and disappeared into the trees. Maybe Clyde's not so bad after all. He had his rifle with him, but he didn't try to shoot me. There's no way to find him in these mountains."

One of the deputies who had been trained as a medic began to try emergency first aid on Leland, but it was too late to do any good, and he was obviously dead. At the sheriff's direction, a makeshift stretcher was formed from a blanket found in the cabin and four deputies started back down the slope carrying Leland, preceded by another with the mine detector.

Grindle, Ron, and I sat on the front porch while the two sheriffs began to search the cabin. It was now dark and I was hungry, thirsty, and totally exhausted. I got up enough energy to go into the cabin and find some water to drink. Clyde had rigged a tank on the roof and a makeshift gravitational system collected rainwater that ran down a pipe along the wall. There were several battered pitchers and old plastic containers he used to collect the water for drinking, cooking, and maybe even washing, although the cabin didn't smell like it. I brought a plastic bottle full of water back to Grindle and Ron. When I looked at them, I started to laugh.

Grindle turned and said, "What the hell are you laughing at, Okie?"

"We sure as hell don't look like the winning team." This brought a laugh out of Ron and even a small smile out of Grindle. "By the way, Grindle, you better comb your hair and wash your face before your photo op. We sure don't want you to look bad for the cameras, and incidentally, thanks for shooting Leland. I must admit, that was a great shot, and it may have saved my ass."

Ron then looked at me and said, "Say, Snake, let's go back and get those packs." That really cracked me up, and I started laughing almost hysterically from a combination of exhaustion, excitement, and just the sheer good feeling of being alive and not lying at the bottom of some cliff or being carried down the mountain with one of Leland's bullets in me.

CHAPTER 57

We waited on the front porch until Sheriff Checker came out and told us the results of the search. They had found all kinds of weapons, including explosives and dynamite. There was an extensive library of right-wing literature, paramilitary instruction books, and scientific works on manufacturing bombs and other explosive devices, and all kinds of furs and skins of various animals, which Clyde trapped. But Sherman and Clyde were clearly gone.

We knew Clyde was running in the mountains and that the chances of finding him were small. Where Sherman had gone was anybody's guess. He seemed to always be able to disappear just in time. Further, he was not really a fugitive. There were no charges against Sherman and little evidence he had been involved in any kind of felony, although it was almost certain he had taken part in the beating of the highway patrolman. It looked like Sherman was a general who knew how to maneuver his troops, but stay behind the lines when it came to getting caught for any crimes.

I managed to pick myself up and stagger down the hill to where the sheriff and the others had left their vehicles at the abandoned mine. At least it was downhill, although my quads hurt so badly there was little relief from going down instead of up. I slumped into the backseat of one of the county's SUVs and began to doze off in spite of the rough road down the side of the mountain. After drinking some more water, I began to feel a little better by the time we reached Ouray. I was hungry, but all I could think about was rest and went immediately into my motel room, threw myself on the bed, and fell asleep still wearing my clothes.

When I woke up the next morning I turned on the TV, and sure enough, the news was all about the shoot-out at Clyde's cabin. Leland, of course, was dead, Ron had apparently gone home when we reached Ouray, and I had passed out at the motel, but Grindle had somehow rallied. He was interviewed on TV and was doing his best John Wayne performance. He had come up with a black cowboy hat and had managed to get himself cleaned up before his photo op. To hear his story, he was a combination of Edmond Hillary and Wyatt Earp. When asked about Ron's part in the adventure, Grindle simply described him as a guide. He did mention he was accompanied by a deputy sheriff from Oklahoma, a real concession for Grindle. He reminded me of my days as a backup quarterback watching the players who had starred in the game being interviewed on TV afterward.

I took a hot shower, put on clean clothes, and went into the motel restaurant where I drank a vat of coffee and downed a stack of pancakes, two eggs, bacon, and biscuits. The *Denver Post* and the *Rocky Mountain News* both featured pictures of Grindle. The *Denver Post* had also found an old mug shot of Leland. Clyde was described as a reclusive outlaw. Sheriff Jackson, Sheriff Checker, Ron, and I were mentioned near the end of the article. However Grindle had clearly succeeded in making himself the hero of the entire incident.

While I was eating breakfast, Sheriff Checker came in to the restaurant to tell me I needed to file a detailed report at Sheriff Jackson's office. Even though I knew Leland got what he deserved, I was glad it was not my bullet that caused his death. It seems Don Ed was having an influence on me, whether I liked it or not.

I wanted to say good-bye to Ron before we left town, so we drove by Ron's house and talked to his wife. She advised us that Ron had gone to work that morning at 7:00 a.m., just the way he always did, and was out with a surveying crew somewhere in the mountains. Somehow this didn't surprise me, even though I was aching all over and barely able to hobble around stiff-legged.

We went to the county courthouse, where Sheriff Jackson's office was located. The sheriff had already talked to Mike, who had gone to the airport in Montrose to make sure the plane would be serviced and ready for our flight back to Oklahoma.

I sat down at a word processor and typed out my report using the briefest and most perfunctory cop terms. After I finished and gave the report to Sheriff Jackson, I told him Ron ought to receive some kind of citizen's medal or award for what he had done. Sheriff Jackson agreed. About that time, Grindle came swaggering into the sheriff's office. He was still wearing his black cowboy hat, jeans, and cowboy boots.

"I'm glad to see you're up and around, Snake. After I had to drag you up and down that mountain, I didn't know if you'd be able to walk around at all."

"I just got in from the dance, Grindle. I had to take your girlfriend home before I came down to type up my report. She told me you hadn't been able to take care of her, so I thought I'd do you the favor."

I could see Sheriff Jackson crack a smile, and a few chuckles and hoots came from the other deputies.

"Sheriff, I'd like to organize a search for Clyde," Grindle said.

This really caused the other deputies to laugh and hoot.

"Grindle, our best chance to catch Clyde is to wait until next fall when it snows and he's got to come down out of those mountains. I'm not gonna waste time, effort, or manpower chasing Clyde. We have about as much chance of catching him in the mountains as we do of catching a ghost. On top of that, the most we could charge him with would be harboring a fugitive, and I'm not even sure we could make that stick. He'd say he didn't have any idea that those fine patriotic citizens who were visiting him had ever violated any law at all, not to mention the laws of the corrupt federal government and the bankrupt state of Colorado. You've had your fifteen minutes of fame. Your next important assignment is going to be as security guard at the Fourth of July picnic."

Grindle puffed up like a big toad and responded, "The way I know these woods and can handle the mountains, I could go in there by myself and bring Clyde out in a few days."

"To make it clear, Grindle, don't try that unless you want to look for another job. I'm still in charge around here, and I'm sayin' we're lucky we got Leland with nobody being killed or hurt. You're damn lucky you had Ron to take you up there and Snake to back you up. I don't know why that dog wanted to eat Snake instead of you, or why Leland's bullet hit your vest, but you came out smelling like a rose. Don't push it. Just prepare your report. Then you can take the rest of the day off so you can figure out how to get on TV again before all the media people get tired of this story."

The two sheriffs sat down and decided what to do next. They figured there was enough evidence against Clyde to try and get the Colorado DA to charge him and issue a warrant for his arrest. Even though he could hide in the mountains, he'd have to come down sometime for supplies, and maybe with a little luck, he might get caught. They also decided to put out Sherman's picture among law enforcement agencies in hopes that he might be spotted, even though neither one of them was quite sure what could be done with him if he was found. After they finished their conference, Sheriff Checker and I shook hands all around and prepared to leave.

I went over to Grindle and offered my hand. Grindle did take it, shook my hand, and even said, "Thanks for backing me up, Okie. You're pretty good cop, for a smart-ass."

Mike was waiting for us at the airport, and after the sheriff downed a Dramamine, we climbed in the Baron and headed back for Oklahoma.

CHAPTER 58

As soon as I got home, I called Dawn, wanting to share every detail of the climb and the shoot-out. It was great to have someone to talk to. The initial excitement of our relationship was being replaced by the routine of seeing each other on a regular basis, and yet I was always anxious to spend time with her, eager to tell her how the things in my life were going, and to hear about her son and the store. There was clearly a strong pull developing between us as we each became more dependent on the other for companionship and, of course, sex. Some things need explaining, but since relationships between men and women are largely inexplicable, it is better to simply enjoy a good one if you can find it and forget the ones that don't work. Explanations probably won't help matters one way or another.

I tried to portray my role in the climb and the shoot-out as an understated hero, but Dawn caught me out more than once with a wicked smile or a pointed comment, although I think she was concerned for my safety.

"I thought all you sheriffs did was sleep in your car and give speeding tickets. I'm impressed."

"Aw shucks, ma'am. I just did my duty as I saw it."

"Ron sounds like the real hero to me. He didn't have to go."

"I think he did it for the challenge, and maybe just to make Grindle sweat."

"Grindle came through, though. You'll have to give him that."

"That's true, but you'd like Ron. You minorities get along."

"You betchum, White Man. We know how to skin you tourists just like we used to skin the buffalo."

"You've got a wise mouth for a squaw. Maybe I ought to have more than one woman, like a true chief."

"Don't push it. You're only a deputy sheriff, but I've missed you while you were playing cowboys and bandits. Why don't you come over here and prove you're good for something besides giving speeding tickets."

And that's just what I did.

CHAPTER 59

I was looking up baseball trivia on the Internet when Don Ed walked into the sheriff's office.

"Snake, I've got a motion docket in Hobart. Why don't you drive me over to court? It will give us a chance to talk about Crankcase."

"What if I say I'm busy, Judge?"

"I don't think you want to sit in jail while I drive over to Hobart and conduct a motion docket and set bond on your contempt of court charge," Don Ed responded with a wry smile.

"Now you're talkin' language I can understand. I guess you'll authorize a mileage reimbursement for me for helping to bring justice to Kiowa County."

We got in my car and headed south out of Cordell toward Hobart.

"Since I have the judge with me, I guess I can speed all I want."

"No, you can speed all I want. Hold it to about seventy-five."

"Tell me where the case stands, Judge."

"First of all, it's set for trial next month, so there's pressure on both sides. The blood test was ordered by the court, and the DA knows the results. He reluctantly agrees that this does create some defense for Crankcase. He's willing to drop the death penalty request, but he still wants a guilty plea on first-degree murder and a life sentence. It would be hard for him to agree to a plea for less than murder one. A life sentence is his first offer, and personally I think the public defender can get him down to twenty years."

"What about Butterfly and Crankcase's alibi testimony?"

"That's really tricky. The public defender will have to reveal the name of any alibi witness to the prosecution before the trial starts. Once he discloses Butterfly's name, the DA's office will have the police go out and question her about her testimony. If she tells them she doesn't remember anything about the incident, we haven't really gained very much. Even if she suddenly developed total recall, the police and the DA are going to figure they can rip her apart since she was a drug addict and was high when she was with Crankcase. The other side of the coin is that knowing that she exists does make Crankcase's story more credible. It's tricky."

"Is there anything more I can do to help?"

"Maybe. Do you think you could get Butterfly to refuse to talk to the police? Then at least they'll think she's going to be a hostile witness. It might give us a little more leverage with the plea bargain. It will take some guts on her part. The police and the DA will bully her to make her tell them what her testimony will be at trial. They might even subpoena her before a judge and try to take her deposition or file a motion to exclude her testimony from the trial, if she won't cooperate. Do you think she'd at least help to the extent of not talking to the police or DA?"

"Judge, I don't know. She's a strange cat. She likes Mike, and I think she likes me. It's because of my positive aura and my good karma, not my looks or my personality."

"Well, thank God we're not relying on your looks or your personality, or we'd all be in deep shit."

"Seriously, Judge, I don't mind asking her, but there are things about her that make me believe she is Lucas' daughter in a lot of ways. That means that she'll definitely save her own ass first. But who knows? She's not a person I would want to predict. You'll have to tell me exactly what you want, and then I'll ask for her help."

"Let me think about the best strategy. We've got another problem, and that's Crankcase. Now that he's in prison, he's become a hard-ass, and he's not sure he wants to plead to anything. I'm sure the PD could get him to plead to theft, illegal use of a credit card, or possession of drugs, but I don't know about murder. I thought I'd stopped worrying about these kinds of cases, but I guess you were right, Snake. It's still in my blood."

"Yep, Judge, you're just like an old rodeo cowboy who can't quit. Maybe I ought to write a song about that. I'll work on that while you hear all these lawyers wrangle over those motions you guys love so much. I don't know what's going to happen to your profession if somebody ever figures out how many angels can dance on the head of a pin. I do know that no two lawyers are ever going to agree to a final decision on that, or any other issue."

When we got to the county courthouse in Kiowa County, the judge went into the courtroom to handle his motion docket. I went in the judge's chambers, and before the idea left me entirely, I took a yellow legal pad and wrote, "Hey, Old Cowboy."

HEY, OLD COWBOY

Hey, Old Cowboy
can you saddle up and ride
one more time
down along the border line?

Can you still ride
and shoot
and chase those cows
and throw a loop?

Let me tell you, son
there's still some fight
in this old rooster
even though I ain't what
I use'ter.

I can still ride
and shoot
and there's plenty of fight
in this old galoot.

Don't Never Shoot Short

If you hire me
I'll be up before the sun and
you'll get a day's work
when a day is done.

I've fought Indians
and bandits too
and there's nothing that
I'd rather do.

'Cause a cowboy's
life is all I know
and I've punched cows
in rain and snow.

'Cause I've rode hard
and I've rode far
I've shot a man
And I've killed a b'ar.

'Cause I can't stand
to stay at home
when there's still
country out there to roam.

I want to see sights
I've never seen
in places that may be
fine or mean.

So cut me out
A horse that can run
And I'll chase your cows
and call it fun.

If I die
on the prairie out there
just bury me
with a cowboy prayer.

When you dig my grave
for my last sleep
do me a favor
and plant me deep.

So the wolves that howl
won't eat my bones
and my resting place
will be my last home.

Out there somewhere
where no one knows
and no one comes
and no one goes.

So I'll saddle up and ride
one more time
and I'll think again
that the world's still fine.

Before we started back to Cordell, I read it to the judge. He got a kick out of the poem, and I told him I'd type it up and give him a copy.

"Someday, Snake, you ought to write a book. I'd buy a copy. I might even read it."

That was about as big a compliment as Don Ed ever paid anyone.

CHAPTER 60

Red had the TV on in the office. He was waiting for the early football game to start and the news was on. I usually watched the news, but wasn't paying much attention, until a story came on about the kidnapping of an American who was working on an oil rig in Columbia.

They had pictures of government troops and what they described as guerilla troops as well. The story continued on to show a reported drug lord who was supposed to have direct ties to the guerillas who had kidnapped the American.

The drug lord was shown walking from his heavily fortified mansion to his armored Mercedes. Marching along next to him was a big, bull-necked man in Army fatigues, carrying a conspicuous sidearm.

"Damn it, Red, that's Sherman. The bastard is down in Columbia with some drug lord."

"I'll be a pluperfect son of a bitch, you're right, Snake. What can we do about it?"

"Probably not a thing, but we need to tell Chubby. At least we know it's a waste of time to look for him in Colorado."

We told the sheriff about seeing Sherman on TV. He didn't have any ideas, although he was going to inform Sheriff Jackson and Glen Smith. Just seeing Sherman made me a little uneasy. Even though he was thousands of miles away, I had a feeling I'd be running into him again sometime.

CHAPTER 61

A few days later I heard from Crankcase's public defender. He was still trying to negotiate a plea with the district attorney but needed to talk to Crankcase personally to determine what sort of a deal Crankcase might accept. He asked me to meet him at Granite so he could be filled in on the details and meet with Crankcase at the same time.

The same fat guard ushered me into one of the attorney conference rooms at the prison. The public defender, Gene Green, was already there. He was a middle-aged, black man whose hair was beginning to turn gray. A little overweight, Gene wore a cheap, ill-fitting suit and was smoking a cigarette. Don Ed liked him and thought he was a conscientious and capable criminal defense lawyer.

"Deputy, glad to meet you. I understand they call you Snake."

"That's right, but I'll answer to almost anything."

"I'm going to have them bring Crankcase in to see us in a few minutes. Before we talk to Crankcase, I want to know exactly what you have found out about the alibi witness. I haven't told the DA about the witness yet. I'm holding that information back until I see what his best offer for a plea is based on the different blood found on the victim's clothing. I'm afraid it may not matter, anyway. Crankcase says he's an innocent man and isn't going to plead to anything. The problem we have with these guys is that they gain status in the joint by being a tough guy. Telling the law to go to hell makes them big shots with the other prisoners. On the other hand, I'm not sure Crankcase will really want to roll the dice to see if he can beat the death penalty."

I filled the public defender in on Butterfly/Angel. Gene asked me a lot of questions to try to see whether she would actually testify to at a trial. After he got all the information from me he asked the guard to bring Crankcase in for a conference.

"My man, Gene, and my man, Snake. Good to see you. I'm ready for you to walk me right out of this place. I'm tired of these white mother fuckers ragging on my skinny, black ass. You hear what I'm sayin'?"

"That's what I came to talk to you about, Eldridge. You're not walking out of anywhere. You may, however, be able to save your life," Gene said.

"Don't go talkin' to me about no guilty plea. I'm innocent. You told me about the blood, and I know that proves that I'm innocent. I want off and I want out. You hear what I'm sayin'?"

"It's not that simple, Eldridge. I've got to defend you and present your case. I've got to advise you what your chances are if you go to trial and what sort of deal the district attorney would make if you plead guilty. I brought Snake along to fill in any details about the alibi witness that might help you understand what can be done for you and what can't."

"I'm hearin' you say you found that little white bitch can get me off by tellin' where I was when the man got his self killed."

"No, that's not exactly right," Gene replied. "We found somebody who fits your description. She doesn't know you, she doesn't know where you were, and she doesn't know what happened. She can't prove whether you were telling the truth. But she does exist, and that's more than the DA would have ever believed. We may be able to use her to get you a better deal, but don't forget that she's a drug addict who was on drugs when all this happened and says she doesn't remember a damn thing."

"Well you just haul her lyin', white ass into court and make her talk. Ain't that what you're paid to do?"

"Listen to me again, Eldridge. If she won't verify your story, she might do you more harm than good."

Turning to me, Crankcase said, "What the hell good are you, Sheriff, if you can't make that bitch tell the truth? You let me out of here and let me talk to her, and I won't have no trouble getting her to talk. You hear what I'm sayin'?"

"I probably wouldn't offer her drugs or money like you would, Crankcase, since that's against the law. Besides, I'm not sure if she really does remember anything. Her mind is so screwed up by all that dope you sold her that she may really not have any memory of what happened."

"You mother fuckers have to get me out of here, you hear what I'm sayin'? The Nazis have a contract on me. That's the word. They heard I was talkin' to the sheriff here and one of those peckerwoods was the one he shot, big old mean mother fucker name of Cedric. That sorry bastard is dangerous to my health. They're figurin' I'm doin' somethin' for the law. The brothers know better, but those Nazi mother fuckers are dumb and crazy. You hear what I'm sayin'?"

"Let me tell you, Eldridge. I can work a deal for you, I can get the DA to drop the request for the death penalty, I can get him to go for life or maybe even thirty years, but you're gonna have to plead to get that deal. If we go to trial, he'll seek the death penalty. The blood evidence is important. It might work, but there's no guarantee. You've been to trial once, and you know what can happen. You're still a criminal, you're still black, and you're still a drug dealer. If you know any jurors that are gonna like you, then you know a hell of a lot more about court than I do," Gene said.

"Just stop right there, Mr. Public Defender. You're my free lawyer, and I want your free ass defending me and not makin' no deal with no mother fuckin' DA. You and the sheriff here can just get that damn witness and stick it up her ass 'til she says what she has to say to get me off. What you gonna do about savin' me from the Nazis?"

"We're gonna need to talk about this again, Eldridge," Gene responded. "In the meantime, I'll see how soon I can get you moved down to the Oklahoma County jail. The county jail's full and the

Oklahoma County sheriff won't want you down there until right before the trial, but I'll see what I can do. In the meantime, you think about what your life is worth and about twelve white, church goin' citizens sittin' there and lookin' at a skinny ass nigger that sells drugs, had the dead mans credit card, and who left his fingerprints on the cab. I don't care how many witnesses I call on to help you, you aren't gonna get white or clean before the trial."

Gene then called for the jailer, who took Crankcase back to his cell. We stayed and discussed the case for a few minutes longer. Gene asked me to talk to Butterfly to see if she would help by at least refusing to talk to the DA or the police. As a law enforcement officer, this put me in a real conflict, asking someone not to cooperate with an investigation, but I knew I'd do it for Don Ed. I asked Gene to keep his mouth shut about my role in the case. He promised me he would, and I accepted his word based on Don Ed's assessment. I left Granite knowing I'd have to talk to Butterfly, but had no idea what her response was going to be.

CHAPTER 62

The land department of Chesapeake Oil Company called me with an assignment. Chesapeake was one of the independent oil and gas companies I did leasing and title work for in western Oklahoma. The job sounded easy. The company wanted me to check the title on Morford's farm. Chesapeake was interested in drilling a deep gas well on the property and needed to know who owned the minerals for leasing purposes.

My job required I check the records, though I already knew Lucas's bank owned the farm and the minerals, but just knowing something isn't good enough for oil and gas lawyers. They don't work that way. Oil and gas lawyers are some of the biggest nitpickers and flyspeckers in the world. Their life revolves around the infinitesimal details of complicated legal documents. These lawyers enjoy the same sort of minds possessed by computer nerds. They are the kind of people who get off on the arcane language in ancient instruments and absolutely go euphoric over finding some minute discrepancy in a title document. Even though I was certain the bank owned all of Morford's minerals by way of foreclosure, I still had to verify ownership from the records. Strange things happen when it comes to the ownership of oil and gas minerals.

The records showed that Morford's farm had been in his wife's family all the way back to the original land grant. Her grandfather had homesteaded part of the property. Later he added to it, so that he owned eight hundred acres, all of which had been inherited by her father. Her father died, and Mrs. Morford had inherited his interest, along with a brother, who it appeared was also dead. Mrs. Morford had also died. Both the grandfather and the father's estate had been probated in Washita County. The wills in both of these estates were complicated, old documents, single-spaced and typewritten. The final decrees in the probate proceedings used terms that were no longer seen, even in legal documents.

Of course, in checking the records, I found the mortgage signed by the Morfords to Lucas' bank. Then there was the judgment in foreclosure and a copy of the sheriff's deed conveying the farm to the bank.

I worked through all these records, and using the form furnished to me by Chesapeake, I carefully listed the dates of all of the transactions and filings and identified the grantors, grantees, beneficiaries, the type of document filed, and the book and page numbers. After I had finished my "take off," not being too busy, I decided to go back and read the grandfather and the father's wills and final decrees. There is a certain fascination in these old documents, even to a layman. It's like reading a family history or a family tree. I didn't understand all of the legal technicalities, but I thought it might be interesting to see what had happened to the Morford family. As it turned out, it was more than interesting.

Historically, farmers and ranchers in western Oklahoma have had a fanatical attachment to their land. These people, who live off of the land, respect it and want to see that it stays in their family for future generations. In order to accommodate this mindset, years ago, lawyers employed what is called a life estate. A life estate means a person only owns the right to the property for their life. When there is a life estate, there is also a remainder estate. The remainder estate is the interest of the person who owns the property after the death of the life estate owner. The idea was to leave a life estate to one generation and a remainder estate to following generations. Sometimes there were even successive life estates left to succeeding generations. All of this could lead to confusing and conflicting ownerships between generations and members of a family, particularly if there were premature deaths in any generation which spread the title out to the children of various life estate owners. These complex plans for the distribution of estates became even more complicated when the mineral interests were treated differently from the surface. Such a scheme could be even further confused when different heirs executed oil and gas leases to different oil companies, making the title to the mineral interests even more complex, as beneficiaries died and generations passed.

Both Mrs. Morford's grandfather and father had employed the life estate device to attempt to keep their farm in the family. The language of both wills was contorted and difficult to understand. Additionally, both of the deceased Morfords had treated the minerals differently than they had the surface, for purposes of distribution under the will. I knew this was going to be a title where the attorney would require copies of the documents in both of these estates, so I had the clerk make certified copies to send to Oklahoma City along with my "take off." All of my work was then bundled up and put into a UPS package for delivery to the land department of Chesapeake in Oklahoma City. Just before I sealed the box, I got a funny feeling that something was left out that should be included, but could think of nothing and, finally, closed the box.

In spite of the complicated pattern of succession of the Morford minerals, I had no doubt the bank owned all of these mineral interests through the foreclosure. After all, Floyd was a meticulous lawyer and the foreclosure had surely captured all of the Mr. Morford's interest for Lucas and his bank.

Doing these title checks was interesting but awfully dry work, and I called Mike to see if he'd meet me for a beer. He was out of town, probably with Butterfly, so I headed home for another night alone.

That night, something was bothering me. I wasn't sure what it was, but couldn't sleep and was restless, so I was up walking around the house listening to CDs on my stereo. I turned on a Mary Chapin Carpenter CD. Listening to her songs, sung with such a clear and perfect voice settled me down some.

After awhile I was finally able to get to sleep, but slept only lightly and when I woke, realized what was bothering me. Morford's wife had died, but there was no record of any probate of her estate. I got up, got dressed, and headed back to the courthouse. As soon as the courthouse opened, I went to the court clerk's office. It is not uncommon for an estate to be probated in court and the final decree properly filed with the district court clerk but never delivered to the county clerk for filing in the real estate records. However, in this case there was no record of any probate of Mrs. Morford's estate in the court clerk's office, either.

This seemed significant enough to call the land department at Chesapeake and give them the information. The title lawyer's secretary took the information and said she'd let me know if they needed anything else.

CHAPTER 63

A few days later, Chesapeake's title attorney reached me at the office.

"Thanks for the tip on Mrs. Morford, Snake. It is important that she is dead. Do you know if the Morfords had any children?"

"I don't know for sure. It seems like they had children. Red will know. Hang on just a minute...Red, did the Morford's have any children?"

"Yea, there's a grown son named Joe. He works at the grain elevator at Rocky and drives a truck part-time. I think they had a daughter, too. She may live over in Elk. I can find out, if you need to know for sure."

"Yes, it looks like they have one, and maybe two, living children. What's the deal?" I said to the attorney

"I have to do a little more studying and legal research, but it looks like the bank didn't foreclose all of the mineral interests that are owned by the Morford family. It may be that the Morford children still own all, or at least part, of the minerals."

"I can't believe Floyd would have failed to pick up all the minerals in the foreclosure. He just doesn't make those kinds of mistakes."

"I know, and that's why I want to check it out further before I render an opinion to the company. Also, I need to call Floyd as a courtesy. We've done a lot of business with his clients, and I want to give him a chance to straighten this out if I've missed something or if a document was misfiled by the clerk. Go ahead and see if you can locate Morford's children, and I'll call you back as soon as I have an opinion on the title."

I hung up the phone and turned toward Red with a huge smile on my face.

"What the hell's so funny, Snake? I can't imagine there's anything about that boring work you do that could possibly be considered a joke."

"It looks like the joke maybe on our close, personal friend, Duane Lucas. It couldn't happen to a nicer guy."

A few days passed and I received another call from the title attorney.

"Snake, I've reexamined all the documents and I've talked to Floyd. It's my opinion that the minerals under the Morford farm are owned by Morford's children. Whoever drafted the note and mortgage misconstrued one of those crazy old wills that had that confusing life estate language and didn't have the children mortgage their interest."

"I don't believe it. How could Floyd have screwed up the ownership in the foreclosure? I've never head of him making that kind of mistake."

The title attorney started laughing. "That's the funny part. Floyd didn't make the mistake. He just about shit when I told him what I had found. I never heard Floyd cuss like that before. It seems that Lucas was trying to save money, so he hired some greenhorn attorney over in Elk City who just got out of law school to do legal work for the bank. According to Floyd, the lawyer charged about half what Floyd's firm did for the same work. Lucas saved money all right, but he sure didn't save the minerals. If we hit a well out there, this could be a million-dollar mistake. Floyd's not responsible. Lucas only hired him after he realized there were going to be problems with Morford in the foreclosure case. The young lawyer prepared all the documents and pleadings before Floyd was ever hired. Anyway, I'm drawing up leases for Morford's children. There'll be a nice lease bonus for them and of course a royalty interest. We want to get the leases signed so that we can go out there and stake a well. The company thinks it's a great gas prospect, and we figure gas prices are going up right away."

"I couldn't be happier. Get the leases to me and I'll go talk to Morford children. They're going to be completely dumbfounded. I'm sure I won't have any trouble getting the leases signed. Who gets to break the news to Lucas?"

"Oh, I'll probably give him a call after you get the leases signed and let him know we need to negotiate some surface damages. Why he might even get a few thousand dollars out of us for a road and the rig site. Is that what we call 'chump' change, Snake?" the lawyer asked, laughing at his own joke.

What I really wanted was a chance to see Lucas' face when he found out he didn't own the Morford minerals. I hoped that young lawyer in Elk City had plenty of malpractice insurance, because Lucas sure wasn't the kind of person who was just going to let this drop. He'd sue everybody, and Chesapeake was in for a hell of a fight before they got a chance to drill a well on the Morford farm.

My next job really was easy. I received the leases by courier that afternoon and headed down to Rocky to find Morford's son, Joe Jr. Sure enough, he worked at the grain elevator and was just closing up when I arrived. I had trouble convincing him he owned any interest at all in his parents' farm. He wanted me to talk to his dad before he took the lease bonus and signed the lease. I showed him the draft for the bonus of $16,000 and told him I had the same payment for his sister. He just kept shaking his head and staring at the draft until I got him to call his father. After a brief conversation on the phone, I agreed to follow him back to Cordell to the house where Morford was living so we could talk about the lease. Joe drove his old pickup truck, and I followed him in my car.

Morford was living with a cousin in a small, wooden-frame house in Cordell. When we arrived he was standing in the front yard, dressed in biballs and no shirt. When he saw me his eyes narrowed with obvious suspicion. In his mind I was the law and therefore the enemy.

One thing growing up in Oklahoma teaches you is to meet a problem head on, so that's the way I approached Morford.

"Mr. Morford, I'm not here as a sheriff. I work for Chesapeake Oil Company. They are totally reputable. You can check it out if you want, but they are offering your kids a fair deal. Best of all, they are ready to drill a well right away. If they hit, you'll have an income for the rest of you and your kids' lives."

"Why don't Lucas own my farm? That son of a bitch stole it from me in court. Even the general told me that."

"It's complicated as all hell. The lawyers will have to work it out, but in the meantime I've got drafts for your boy and your daughter for $32,000, and they've got a chance of owning three-sixteenths of a lot of oil and gas money. You've got nothing to lose and everything to gain."

"We get the money no matter what happens in court?"

"That's right. You sign the lease and the money's yours, plus the shot at the well."

"We need to talk. You wait here." With that, Morford and his son turned and went into the house, and I was left standing in the hot sun in the front yard. Some time passed before they returned.

"Give me that lease and let me look at it," Morford said. He took the lease, a legal-sized printed document, replete with fine print and difficult to understand. He looked at it much like a monkey examining the outside of a coconut.

"Where does it say what you told us, Deputy?"

I pointed out the typed-in language that showed the royalty interest and the lease bonus, as Morford and his son looked over my shoulder.

Morford's son then proved he was a lot smarter than he looked.

"Okay, you tell your company I'll sign, but only if they agree to start a well within one year, not three, like it says, otherwise I'll just hang on to my interest and see if some other company wants to lease. My sister will do the same thing. I want it in writing."

I pulled out my cell phone and called the company to see if I could change the lease. I managed to get hold of the head of the land department, and he said to go ahead and agree to a one year lease. I wrote the language in the lease by hand and Joe initialed it and signed the lease. He called his sister and she agreed to drive over and sign the next day.

The company and the Morfords were happy, but I was even happier. All I got paid was my day rate, but that wasn't anything compared to knowing that Duane Lucas had finally lost out on one of his shylock deals.

CHAPTER 64

Dawn and I were sitting in her backyard watching her son and one of his buddies play catch. For a ten-year-old, her son, Buddy, had a pretty good arm. He could throw the ball clear across the yard with some accuracy.

"Kid's got a good gun on him. He may have a future in baseball."

"What about you, Snake? What's in your future? Everybody around here wonders when you're going to leave for the big city. You're from here all right, but you just don't fit, fancy education and good-looking. Don't get a big head, but what are you doing here, and are you stayin' or goin'?"

"I don't know myself. After the bank failed I had nothing to do. I figured I'd stay around for awhile, and I did. I guess you'd say I'm a temporary, permanent resident of western Oklahoma, which, summed up, means I don't know what I want to do when I grow up."

"You'll never grow up, but you will have to make up your mind one day. I can't see you settling for a deputy sheriff's job the rest of your life."

"At least I know a few things I don't want to do, like banking, no moneygrubbing, no ass kissing, and no brownnosing."

"I guess you'll just die poor, then—unless you strike oil. What about the oil business? You know a lot about it."

"Maybe. Or maybe I could help you open up a chain of stores. Dawn's Delis or Dawn's Delights or even Delicious Dawn's."

"Yeah, but seriously, where are you going, and where are we going, and are we going together?" Dawn looked serious when she asked.

"I know I want to be with you. I don't know why that would change. Isn't that good enough for now?"

She looked at me and with a smile and theatrical sigh and responded, "I guess—for now."

As to the present, I was being truthful. As to the future, I really didn't have a clue.

CHAPTER 65

It was Saturday morning. I was in the café waiting for Red, having just run ten miles. The climb to Slidin' Clyde's cabin had confirmed there was a reason to stay in shape, although I didn't expect another adventure like that one to come along any time soon. A patented Oklahoma wind was blowing, and I was tired from fighting the five miles back to town into a mostly twenty-mile-an-hour south wind.

While I drank a cup of almost decent coffee, I read the Saturday edition of the Daily Oklahoman. A journalism critic had once named the Oklahoman as the worst major daily newspaper in the United States. I thought that assessment was a little unfair. The editorials were the worst I had ever read. They were a largely indecipherable stream of theocratic, right-wing nonsense. The paper, however, had a decent sports page and did a fair job of covering local and state news.

Red was late, so I read the front page, the sports page, and glanced at the stock market. I began to work my way through the other news when I saw a small article in a box on page seven of the newspaper. The caption read, "Prisoner Murdered." I noticed the byline was Granite. What I read gave me an instantly bad feeling. The article recited that the guards had found a prisoner, Eldridge Case, beaten to death in the prison shower. The article mentioned that Case was a murder defendant, awaiting retrial in Oklahoma City. It recited a few facts about his original murder case and concluded that the authorities thought Case's murder was racially motivated.

Crankcase had been right—his fears were well-founded. Cedric or some of Cedric's pals had done the job on Crankcase. I sure didn't

231

feel responsible, but I was sad. I had convinced myself Crankcase was not guilty of murder. He had more than his share of other faults, and there was nothing much to recommend him as a human being, but he didn't deserve to be killed, and particularly not by Cedric or some other white Aryan brother who represented an even lower form of creature on the food chain. At least Crankcase's death let Butterfly off the hook.

I pulled out my cell phone and called Don Ed at home.

"Judge, I just read in the paper somebody killed Crankcase. It's on page seven of the Daily Oklahoman."

There was a long pause and then Don Ed said, "There are times when I hate the corrections system. We can't keep prisoners safe from each other. I hope they catch the son of a bitch that killed Crankcase, but the chances are pretty damn slim. Can you imagine anybody in prison ratting out another prisoner and then trying to stay alive in that population? What's more likely is that some African American will kill a white guy to get even. It probably won't even be the right white guy."

"Well, Judge, you did everything you could for your client, as usual. You may not have proved that he was innocent to a jury, but you proved it to my satisfaction, for whatever that's worth."

"That and ninety-nine cents will get you a bad cup of coffee, but I do appreciate your work on the case, Snake. I think you've got a future as a private detective, or maybe you're just an expert on women's asses, and that's how you found Butterfly."

"Thanks for the compliment, I think."

"Say, I understand Lucas had a little trouble figuring out who owned the minerals under Morford's farm. He's gotten Floyd to file a motion to re-open the foreclosure case. He has some interesting theories, but I hate to tell him that the statute of limitations has run, and the bank didn't get all the people necessary to sign the mortgage in the first place. Morford won't need the militia to defend this case. Chesapeake hired the best oil and gas firm in Oklahoma City to represent the Morford kids and his wife's estate. They filed a well-written, well-researched brief that I think will convince the judge to deny the motion, even though that old cowboy isn't much of a title lawyer. I also hear Lucas is threatening to sue that young lawyer over in Elk City that did the legal work on the note and mortgage and originally filed the foreclosure case. That won't do Lucas much good. As I understand, the lawyer didn't have malpractice insurance, has already been laughed out of town, and moved to Amarillo, where he's selling used cars. It looks like Lucas is going to enjoy being a gentleman farmer and watching an oil and gas well drilled in the middle of one of his fields. It will interfere with the only crop he ever cared anything about, money."

"You call that a happy ending, Don Ed?"

"Son, you call it anything you like. I call it a joke on someone who deserved it. I'm goin' down to Altus to look at some cattle, and you're invited, but I expect you'd rather go out and play some of that sissy golf you seem to like so much. As far as I can tell, it's just an excuse for riding around in a golf cart drinking beer."

"Enjoy your day, your Honor. I'll pass on the trip, and I'll see you in court."